LET LOOSE

A Hellhounds MC romance

Stacey Broadbent

Published by Stacey Broadbent, Ashburton, NZ
Copyright 2024 © Stacey Broadbent

Proofreading by Spell Bound
Cover image from Deposit Photos
Cover Design by Stacey Broadbent

ISBN: 978-1-0670111-6-1 (paperback)
        978-1-0670111-7-8 (Kindle)

LET LOOSE

A Hellhounds MC romance

Stacey Broadbent

AUTHOR S NOTE

The characters in this story are from New Zealand, therefore UK spelling and terms have been used. Please remember these are not errors, it's just the way we do things here.

Please also note this story contains scenes of a graphic nature and may contain triggers, involving domestic abuse and violence.

HELLHOUNDS MC

PROLOGUE

MATIU

"What've we got here?" Wiping my hands down the front of my overalls, I take in the busty brunette before me. She's got her nose in her phone and her butt leant up against the driver's door of a powder-blue Nissan. She's chewing gum and blowing bubbles that pop against her plump lips every few seconds. I stop in front of her, one eyebrow raised.

She blinks, her eyes shifting from her screen to my face, and lets out an exasperated sigh.

"Gee, I don't know, Einstein. Looks like a car to me."

Behind me, Jeri stifles a chuckle. "She's got you there, bro."

I fold my arms across my chest, jutting my chin. "Shiiit, woman, I can see that. I *mean* what do you need done with it?"

Jeri coughs into his hand, the word *careful* falling out as he walks past. He nods to the brunette then turns to me with a shit-eating grin on his face before stepping into his office.

Whatever, man. I don't need to take advice from a loner on how to handle a woman, especially the feisty ones like this.

She quirks her brow at me, her hip popping out to the side. "*Woman*?"

"That's what you are, ain't it?" I let my gaze traverse her curves with an appreciative grin. "And a fine one at that."

She rolls her eyes, snorting. "In your dreams."

"You can bet on it." I'll definitely be thinking of her while I knock one out tonight. Hell, a chick this hot could stay in the bank for a month, easy.

She clears her throat, her hand falling to her hip. "You work here, or are you just hanging around to perve?"

I hold up my grease-covered palms. "I work. In fact, I'm the best mechanic here."

There's a louder cough from the office, and this time I'm sure I hear the word *bullshit*. It *is* Jeri's business, so I suppose I can let him have that one. "Second best."

She makes a point of looking around. "Could've fooled me. I don't see you doing anything but checking me out." Her tone is deadpan, but there's a hint of a smile on her face.

I step in closer, holding up one finger. "One. You haven't told me what you need yet. And two." I run my tongue along my teeth, leaning back to get another look at her. "I don't see anyone else worth checking out around here, do you?"

She snorts out a laugh. "Smooth, Romeo." Her hand darts out and grabs Zeb by his sleeve, dragging him to her side. He obliges like the puppy dog that he is, his tongue practically hanging out the side of his goddamn mouth. "What about this guy? He's pretty easy on the eye." She smirks, and Zeb grins, puffing his chest out like he's the man. She's going to regret stroking his ego in about five seconds when he's dry humping her leg.

"You hear that? I'm easy on the eye." He curls his thumbs into his chest, nodding his head as if her word is the law. He shuffles closer to her, and she gives him a pointed stare until he moves back to where he was. Dumbarse.

"Don't go getting yourself all worked up there, Zeb. I bet she says that to all the boys."

She taps a finger against her chin. "Funny, I could've sworn I didn't say it about you."

"Ooh." I clutch a hand to my chest, staggering. "Harsh, hot stuff. Why you gotta do me like that?"

She lifts a shoulder, turning back to her phone. "I call it how I see it."

"Oooh," Zeb sing-songs, pointing a greased up finger in my direction as he laughs. Shithead.

9

"Anyway, you going to take a look under the hood, or?" She lets her words hang in the air, her glossy lips pursed. *Fuck.* What I wouldn't give to see them wrapped around my—

"Matty, baby," a high-pitched voice coos along with the clip clop of heels on concrete. I close my eyes, bringing my finger and thumb up to pinch the bridge of my nose. *Not now. Not fucking now.*

Jodi sidles up beside me, her talons wrapped firmly around my arm as she leans her head on my shoulder and peers up at me. "Hey, baby."

I shrug her off, taking a step sideways. "I ain't your baby."

The brunette watches on with interest. Just my fucking luck.

Jodi pouts, running her finger along my jaw until I bat her away. "Don't be like that."

I angle my body toward her, keeping a safe distance away. "And what should I be like, huh?"

She stomps her foot. "I told you, he didn't mean anything to me. It was nothing, baby." She walks her fingers up my arm. "Nothing. I swear it."

"Pssh. Whatever, Jodes. It might not've meant anything to you, but it sure as shit meant something to me." I step back again, raising my hands, palms out towards her. "I'm at work. I don't need this shit." A glance over my shoulder shows Jeri standing in his doorway, his arms folded against his chest. He quirks a brow at me, and I shake my head. I don't need him to step in.

"But who's gonna fix my car?" Jodi whines, drawing my attention back to her.

10

I crane my neck, making a point of looking around the garage that's now empty except for the brunette. The boys have made themselves scarce. "Not anyone here."

"Come on, baby. We were good together, you and me. We can be good again. I promise." She licks her lips. "I'm all yours."

Is she for real right now? Shiiiiit. I wouldn't touch her again with a ten fucking foot pole.

"Not interested."

"But—"

"Oh for fuck's sake." The brunette steps between us, cutting her off. She takes hold of my face, planting her lips on mine. She tastes of mint bubblegum, and her lips are every bit as soft as they look. Her fingers slide around my neck to curl into my hair, and I can't help myself; I pull her in close, my hands splayed across her lower back. When we part, she turns back to Jodi, bringing her thumb up to wipe the corner of her mouth. "He said no, okay? Didn't your mama ever teach you no means no?" She looks her up and down. "Nah, I suppose you're one of those girls who thinks the rules don't apply to you. Am I right?"

I duck my head, fighting back a stupid-arse grin.

Jodi's eyes narrow as she sucks on her teeth. "And who the hell do you think you are, coming in here and stepping in between me and *my* man." Her neck moves side-to-side like one of those bobble head dolls.

The brunette snorts. "Honey, from where I'm standing, he ain't your man anymore. He's moved on, and you should too." She flutters her hand in a downward wave. "Go on. Off you fuck."

"You gonna let her speak to me like that, baby?"

"Yeah, I am. She damn near took the words outta my mouth." I wiggle my fingers in the air. "Bye Felicia."

An enraged growl falls from her lips as she stomps away. She flings her car door open and slams it shut behind her. The tyres screech as she pulls out of the lot, and I can't help but laugh. She always was dramatic.

"You and her? Really?" The brunette eyes me, removing herself from my grip.

I shrug. "She scratched an itch."

"I bet she did." She saunters back towards her car. "Didn't mean to overstep there, but," she glances to where Jodi's car was only moments ago, "girls like that don't seem to get it unless you make it *really* obvious." She rolls her eyes.

"Speaking of that." I waggle my brows. "That was some kiss."

She cocks her head, her hand gesturing up and down her body, like it's a given. "Of course it was."

"Shiiit, woman, you're something else."

She flashes me a grin, a mischievous glint in her black-lined eyes. "I like to think so." She offers me her hand. "I'm Barb."

Barb.

I think I just found the woman of my dreams.

CHAPTER ONE

MATIU

I hear her before I see her. The click of her tongue on the roof of her mouth as she prepares to unleash on me. *Fuck. What have I done this time?*

"Matiu Andre Kawiti, I know you didn't just walk those dirty work boots of yours through my nice clean lounge and kitchen."

Squeezing my eyes closed, I quickly kick off my boots and toss them by the back door. "Sorry, Ma. I'll clean it."

"Damn right you will." She wheezes as she steps into the room behind me, one hand on her hip, the other dabbing a hanky over her face. She tries to give me the eye; the one all mothers dole out to their children, but it quickly dissolves when I grin at her. "Come and give your old mum a hug." She wiggles her fingers, ushering me in.

"Hey, Ma." I have to stoop to wrap my arms around her, and as always, she gives my sides a pinch.

"Not enough meat on your bones, boy." She tsks, pulling away and hobbling towards the fridge. "I know cooking ain't your thing, but you're always welcome here for a meal, you know that." She swivels, giving me a pointed stare until I nod. "And bring that lovely lady of yours too." Turning back to the fridge, she pulls out a Tupperware container and slides it onto the counter. "How is she anyway? Wedding plans going okay?"

The groan slips from my lips before I can stop it, and she throws me a glare, pointing a spoon in my face. "Don't you get all up in arms with me, boy. Planning a wedding is hard work. You better not be leaving it all up to her." She turns away, muttering under her breath. "She's a saint for putting up with the likes of you."

"Shiiit, Ma, tell me how you really feel." I drag a chair out from around the table and spin it to face me, straddling it. "I help plenty."

She side-eyes me, her lips pursed. "Is that so?"

I jut my chin out. "It is. I picked the cake flavour and everything."

A hoarse laugh bursts up from out of her chest.

"What?"

"Of course you did. All you men are the same; think with your stomachs."

14

Grinning, I duck my head. "That's not what Barb says."

Her hand comes out of nowhere, slapping me up the side of my head. "Too much information, boy. You may not be my flesh and blood, but I'm still your mother, and I don't need those kinds of mental images, thank you very much." She chuckles, turning back to the fridge. "Now, what'll you eat? I've got some mussels in here…"

I slap my hands, rubbing them together. "Hell yeah." Barb isn't a fan of seafood unless it's salmon. She reckons it all tastes the same, has a gross texture, and she can't stand the smell. She won't come near me if I've been eating them, so I only get it when I come back home or I'm away with the boys, unless I want to sleep on the couch for the night. Fuck that shit.

"What'd you do?" she asks as I shove the first mussel in my mouth.

"Eh?"

She nods to the container in my hands. It's no secret how Barb feels about seafood.

"I didn't do nothin'."

She folds her arms across her chest.

"I didn't! She's out with Sam getting their dresses pinned or some shit. I dunno." I shrug, scooping out another mussel and downing it in one. It's garlicky and just about the best damn thing I've had in my mouth all day.

Ma's eyes light up like they did when Barb asked her to come along while she tried on dresses a few months back. She tried to play it off as if it was

15

nothing, but I know it meant the world to her. She could never have kids of her own, and she lucked out when I showed up on her doorstep and she took me in, but I guess every woman wants a daughter of their own.

"They've come back in? Oh, I can't wait to see how the final product looks. Even two sizes too big it was gorgeous on her."

"I don't see what all the fuss is about. It's a dress, and a bloody expensive one."

She tsks, shaking her head. "You just wait. The minute you see her, you'll understand."

"If you say so."

"Hello? Mama K?" Holden's voice echoes down the hall.

"In here, love." Ma brushes her hands down her front and turns back to the fridge, pulling out a beer.

Holden swoops in and wraps his arms around her from behind, kissing the back of her head. "Hey, Ma."

"Oh you." She brushes him off, handing him the beer with a grin.

"Well shit, I can see who the favourite is." I roll my eyes, scarfing down another mussel.

"Of course he is." She points to his sock-covered feet. "He follows the rules and doesn't mess up my carpets."

Holden grins, taking a long pull of his beer.

"I said I'd clean it up," I mutter.

"You in the dogbox?" he asks, grabbing the seat across from me.

I push the tub of mussels aside. "I can eat seafood if I want to."

"Mmhmm." Holden smirks, then plunges his fingers into the brine and plucks a mussel out. "That why you're hiding out here eating them?" He pops it into his mouth and swallows, closing his eyes as if to savour the taste.

"Who's hidin'?" I lean back, gripping the back of the chair.

"She's out with Sam, isn't she?"

Ma barks out a laugh, not even bothering to hide her amusement.

I make a show of looking around the room. "Funny, I don't see Darce here anywhere."

"She took the kids to a movie with Cami, but even if she was here, I could still do this, and it wouldn't matter." He takes another mussel and sucks it down. The bastard doesn't even like them that much, he's just doing it to get a rise.

"Yeah, yeah, whatever, man. So I like to keep the peace at home. We all know you'd give up anything if Darce asked you to." He's been in love with her since we were kids, and he even sat by while she married another guy to see her happy. They've been through hell and back to get to where they are now. If anyone understands making sacrifices, it's him.

He holds his hands out. "I don't deny it."

Ma leans her hips against the counter. "And how are those little darlings of yours? Settling in okay?" Darcy and her two children, Bobby and Molly, moved into Holden's bachelor pad a month ago, after her husband, Clay, had driven them off the bank and into a lake. If it hadn't been for Holden, they never would've made it out alive. Clay wasn't so lucky.

"Yeah, they're doing well. Still adjusting, you know?"

"Of course. The poor wee things. I can't imagine how hard it must be to lose a parent so young. Even if he wasn't worthy of the title." She reaches out, placing her hand on his shoulder. "You're doing a great thing for them."

Holden shrugs. "I hope so."

"You are. And Darcy? How's she doing?" Growing up, I'd spent most of my days kicking around with Holden, Cami, and Darcy, so Ma got to know them all pretty well. She even used to joke about me and Cami ending up together. As if that would ever happen. I'm not scared of much, but Cami can be frightening when she wants to be. Bigger balls than most guys I know.

"She still has nightmares, but the counselling is helping, I think."

"It'll take some time. That girl has been through a lot."

"She has."

"Well, I'm always right here if you two ever need a night away. Lord knows when I'll get grandbabies of my own." She gives me a pointed stare, and I hold my hands up.

"Hey, I'm already marrying her. Don't rush me."

"It took you long enough to do that though, didn't it?" She folds her arms across her chest. "I'm not getting any younger, boy."

18

"I can't believe I'm saying this, but I liked it better when we were talking about Holden and how great he is than me knocking up my girlfriend."

"Fiancée," Ma corrects, and Holden smirks as he chugs the last of his beer.

"You want another?" Ma pulls one from the fridge and holds it out to him. Still doesn't offer me one. Whatever.

"Thanks, Mama K, but we really should be off."

I raise a brow. "We should?"

He slaps his hands down on my shoulders and gives me a shove. "Yeah. We've got a bachelor party to plan."

Chapter Two

Barb

"Are you lot ready for this?" My voice cracks as I call from behind the curtain. Never in my wildest dreams did I picture myself in a wedding dress, but here I am. I was never one of those girls who played dress-ups with their mother's gown or had everything all planned out like so many of the girls I knew. I was more of a tomboy, preferring to get my hands dirty with the boys than play mummy and daddy.

"Hurry up already, chickadee. We want to see!"

I can just picture Jen perched on the edge of the seat with her hands clasped in front of her face. When I asked her to come with us, she welled up. I guess never having daughters of her own meant she missed out on all this stuff.

"Jen's gonna need another glass of wine if you don't come out soon," Sam adds, and there's the sound of clinking glasses.

"You three better not be getting wasted without me."

"We wouldn't dream of it. Now get out here so we can see how beautiful you look," Sam gushes.

"Yes, darling. We're dying to see." Mum slurs her words, clearly enjoying the free bubbles a little too much as well.

I suck a breath in through my nose and huff it out my mouth, then hitch up the skirt and step through to the viewing area. There's an audible gasp from all three, and Jen has her hands cupped across her mouth.

"Does it look okay?" I ask, stepping onto the platform and letting the soft fabric fall around my feet. I feel like such a… girl.

"Are you kidding? You look stunning." Sam stands and makes her way to one of the small side tables. "You just need one more thing to complete it." Her finger hovers over a sparkly tiara.

"Not a chance."

"Oh, come on, you only get married once! Don't you want to look like a princess?"

With one hand on my hip, I raise a brow at her. Just because she's Jericho's princess, doesn't mean I want to be one too. "I can honestly say, no I don't. Never have, never will." I turn my attention back to Jen and Mum. "Verdict? Do I pass?"

"I…" Jen's voice breaks, and she shakes her head. "You look like an angel," she manages to say

21

between sniffles. Mum, on the other hand, looks bored out of her tree.

I grimace. "I don't know that that's the look we're going for. An angel marrying a Hellhound?"

Sam laughs, her fingers trailing over several head pieces as she keeps glancing back at me. "It is a little on the nose, I suppose, but who cares? Matiu is going to lose his shit when he sees you."

Mum pulls a face like she's just sucked a lemon before schooling her features and giving me a pinched smile. "You're beautiful, darling."

Sam picks up something that looks like an old-school broach but has a veil attached to it. "How about this?"

"Oh yes," Jen says, clapping her hands. "It's perfect."

I let out a sigh but agree to try the thing, if only to placate them.

Sam pins it to the top of my head and steps back. Her eyes glisten, and she nods. "Yup. That's it. That's the one." She looks to Jen, who is beaming.

"Definitely. Take a look." She points to the mirror behind me. The one I've been too afraid to look in. Picking a dress had been such a hard decision, especially when these two kept picking out everything that made me look like a giant meringue. Thank God for Mama K stepping in and finding one a little less... flouncy. I don't do dresses. Skirts on occasion, but they're not exactly conducive to riding on the back of a motorcycle. Give me a pair of jeans any day.

Jen and Sam both move to either side of me, each taking hold of my hands while I turn around. Mum pours herself another wine, and I wish she'd hand me one. I'm not cut out for this stuff.

I stare into the mirror, blink, then raise my hand to where the veil is perched. The thinly woven fabric somehow frames my face from behind my head, and they're right; I do look kind of angelic. It's… odd, but not entirely unpleasant. I let my gaze travel down the length of my body, and I twist and turn to see myself from all angles. The seamstress had promised it would be perfection once she'd taken it in to my measurements, but I'd had my doubts. Seeing myself in this floor-length gown of pearl, with tiny beads of white embroidered across the bodice and capped sleeves, I can only stare.

"See?" Jen grips my hand in hers. "You're beautiful."

"Ssstunning," Mum slurs before tipping her glass back. I know she's not exactly thrilled about the idea of me marrying Matiu, but she could at least pretend.

Jen tuts, a frown on her face as she watches my mother tilt the near empty bottle of wine this way and that. She gives a slight shake of her head before plastering a smile on her face and giving my arm a squeeze.

"Are we happy?" Monique, the seamstress asks from the side of the room.

"I think so, yeah." I can't quite wrap my head around it. I look almost elegant, something I've never felt in my life, but I think I like it.

23

"No thinking about it, we're definitely happy," Jen says. "You've done a fabulous job, hon."

Monique nods. "Thank you."

"Did you remember—" I start, but she stops me with another nod.

"Of course." She strides towards me, ducks behind, and pinches the small train between her finger and thumb, attaching it to a hidden hook in the back. Sam glances back and grins, and Jen shakes her head.

Monique slides another mirror across the floor and positions it behind and to the side so I can see it in the reflection. There, beneath the train of my dress, is the Hellhounds insignia.

She turns to me with a smile. "The angel has a little Hellhound in her still."

CHAPTER THREE

MATIU

"When you said we had a bachelor party to plan, this is not what I had in mind," I say, taking my seat at the table. Jericho sits in his usual spot at the head, with Stubbs to his left and Holden across from me.

"Hold your horses, we're getting to that. I got you a drink, didn't I?" Holden points to the glass in my hand, and I take a swig.

"Oh you did? Cos I could've sworn it was Zeb who poured this." I tilt my glass in his direction. "What's this all about anyway?"

"Sorry to highjack your plans, but we have business to discuss." Jericho steeples his hands on the table. "It appears our little—"

The door bursts open and Cassian rushes in with a stupid grin on his face and a hickey the size of Mount Taranaki. He pulls out a seat and plonks himself down, saying a quick apology.

"Shiiit, man, you get into a fight with a vacuum cleaner?" I snicker, taking another swig of my drink. Back in the day, that would've been me. Chasing tail and trying to get my end away whenever I had the chance. Back before I met Barb. Before I decided it wasn't a pussy move to put a ring on it, but a damn smart one when you've got a woman like her. I ain't stupid. I know I'm punching well above my weight with Barb. She's a fucking ten, and I'm lucky if I'm a seven.

Cassian's grin spreads across his face as he ducks his head, and Holden wraps his arm around his shoulders, pulling him in and ruffling his hair.

"Gotta get it where you can, right, Cass?" He laughs, letting him go.

Cassian brushes a hand across his jacket, sniffing. "Whatever, man."

"Rookie move," Zeb mutters under his breath.

Cassian leans back in his seat. "At least I'm getting some." He raises his brows and looks Zeb up and down, and I can't help but laugh. The kid's got some balls.

"Hey." Zeb holds his hands up. "I get plenty."

"Pfft, sure." Cassian fists his hand and jerks it back and forth.

"Alright, alright, enough about your love lives. Jesus, you'd think this was a bloody knitting group the way you lot carry on."

Holden raises a brow. "What knitting groups do you go to?"

Jeri shakes his head. "Can we get back to the matter at hand?"

"Sorry, boss," Cassian says, ducking his head.

"As I was saying, our little friends have resurfaced."

Holden leans forward. "The ones from the warehouse?"

Jericho nods. "The ones Clay said weren't dealing in Brookhaven."

"Well shit," I say, folding my arms across my chest. "How'd you know?"

He tips his head towards Zeb. "I've had Zeb out on surveillance. I never trusted Clay to begin with, but then I started hearing rumours, so…" He splays his hands. "I needed to make sure."

Zeb hunches forward, his hands clasped on the table. "Curtis Montgomery and Regan Murphy, also goes by Murph. He's a small-time bookie, regular down at the raceway. Got a coupla heavies who hang off him when he's working the races. Curtis has a secondhand store near Sweetwater Close, but from what I can gather, it's a front for his other dealings. Drugs, weapons…" He glances at Jeri. "And girls."

"Shiiiiiit," I mutter under my breath at the same time as Jeri clenches his fists.

"Here?"

Zeb shakes his head. "Not that I've seen, but that don't mean it ain't happening."

"And Hannibal?"

"Not involved. I've been asking around, and it's only Curtis and Murph's names keep popping up."

"After what he did to Clay, I'm not surprised he's not involved," Holden offers. "I mean, I don't think much of the guy, but he at least seems to be on our side when it comes to distribution."

"What's the plan, old man?" I quirk my brows in Jeri's direction. "I know you've got one."

"The way I see it, these two are bad news and we don't want them hanging around Brookhaven any more than they need to. The betting is fine, but I'm not having them dealing drugs or *anything* around here."

"We bringing Hannibal in on this?" Holden asks. "He was pretty handy at dealing with Clay, pun intended." He sniggers, and the image of Clay with a blade through his finger on this very table comes to my mind. Hellhounds don't do violence unless they have to, but even I have to admit, that was pretty badarse, and maybe even a little admirable. The guy sure knows how to get shit done.

"I think we can handle this one in-house, don't you?" Jeri meets his gaze, then turns to Stubbs, who nods his agreement.

"We got this, son." He leans forward, rapping his knuckles on the table. "Whatever you need, I'm in."

"Zeb and Holden, I want you two on Murph. Make it clear we don't want him dealing. Maybe give him a reminder of what happened to Clay."

Holden's eyes widen. "You want them to think it was us who killed him?"

Jeri tilts his head, the corners of his lips turning down. "What they don't know, won't hurt 'em, and it's more likely he'll listen if he thinks there's even a chance of him swimming with the fishes."

Zeb nods, clicking his tongue against his teeth. "This is gonna be fun."

"Matiu, Stubbs, take loverboy over there with you and sort out Curtis." Jeri points at Cassian. "You're to do what they say, got it?"

Cassian gives a salute. "Course, Jericho."

"I mean it, kid. He's the one we'll have trouble with, and I don't want you getting in over your head."

"Got it. Do as I'm told."

"You better, boy," I say with a grin. "Just ask Stubbs what happens to those who don't follow the rules."

Stubbs waves his disfigured hand in the air, and Cassian's eyes widen. My poker face isn't great at the best of times, and one look at his terrified face has me throwing my head back, laughing. "Shiiit, man, too easy." I shake my head.

"You guys are dicks," Cassian says, but there's a hint of a smile on his face. "I knew that wasn't what happened."

"It's not, but it doesn't mean it can't happen if you're not careful." Jericho gives him a pointed look, and Cassian holds his hands up placatingly.

"No worries, man. I get it."

"Good. I don't think I need to say how crucial this is. We've all got sisters and partners, people we care about who would be his target. I want him out."

CHAPTER FOUR

BARB

"You're home early." I glance up from the magazine I've been flitting through since I got back from the dress fitting. I used to laugh at those women who fawned all over bridal magazines, but now I can't seem to stop myself from at least taking a quick look through each new one I see on the shelves. I've already folded several corners of table settings I want to revisit. *Who even am I right now?*

"Yeah, the stag do planning didn't get very far. Ended up having a meeting with Jeri and the boys." Matiu flops down on the couch beside me, his arm stretched out across the back.

Picking up my glass of wine, I toss the magazine aside and nestle into him. He smells like booze and seafood, but I don't say anything, not when I need to butter him up. Something tells me this isn't the time to let him know my hen's night has become a hen's weekend away. The girls surprised me tonight with a weekend pass to the thermal pools in Hanmer. They've got the whole thing planned out.

Matiu fishes his cigarettes out of his pocket and pinches one between his lips. Throwing the pack onto the table, he reaches into his jacket for his lighter, the orange flame lighting his face up briefly as he inhales. He closes his eyes, a stream of smoke swirling from his nostrils before he speaks. "You remember Clay and the shit storm he created?"

How could I forget? Holden spent many nights round at ours complaining about the way he treated Darcy, Holden's now girlfriend. From what I gather, he was a real piece of shit; beating up on his wife, humiliating her in front of the kids, and running drugs on the side. He was a loser with a capital L.

"I remember."

"The two fuck-knuckles he was dealing through have shown up in Brookhaven again. Fuckin' idiots." He takes another deep drag before dropping the remainder of his cigarette into an ashtray.

"Jeez, they're game. Didn't Clay lose a finger as a warning?" Matiu nods. "There's no cure for stupid, I guess."

He chuckles, the rumble vibrating through his chest and into mine. I snuggle in closer, and his arm curls around my waist.

"How'd it go tonight?" he asks, his thumb strumming up and down my skin. "I bet you looked hot."

I smile against his chest, recalling how his patch looked on my dress. He has no idea I've done it, and I can't wait for him to see. "Not really the look I'm going for, babe, but the girls seem to think you'll like it."

"I bet I'll like it more when it's on the floor." His hand dips lower, cupping my arse.

I slap a hand to his chest. "Such a gentleman."

"Hey, if you wanted a gentleman, you're shit outta luck, lady." His hand lifts and a sharp sting burns my arse cheek followed by the soft caress of his warm hands, soothing the ache and setting my insides on fire. No, a gentleman couldn't do to me what Matiu can. They wouldn't know where to start.

Raising his free hand, he grazes the curve of my jaw as his fingers entwine through the hair at the nape of my neck, tilting my face towards him. His lips are on mine in a fierce kiss. It's urgent, as if he needs my lips to be able to breathe.

I slide my hand up his chest and neck, my thumb stroking along the soft whiskers of his jawline. He grips my arse, pulling me until I'm straddling his lap. His hands slide beneath my top, the rough calluses from working with tools all day rubbing against my skin. With a flick of his fingers, my bra is unhooked. I arch my back, pressing myself into him with a whimper.

He growls against my lips as he palms my breast, his thumb circling the sensitive tip. His other hand snakes up to grip the back of my neck, holding me in place as his tongue delves deeper.

Finding the hem of his shirt, I tug it free from between us and lift it over his head, tossing it to the floor. He makes quick work of mine, adding it to the pile before crushing me to him again. I sigh as his skin meets mine, the ridges of his abs taut against my softness.

He grips my hips, rocking me back and forth, hitting the sweet spot that sets my soul on fire. Tipping my head back, I let out a breathy moan, letting him take control as his lips find my neck, his tongue dipping into the groove of my collarbone. A shiver ripples through me.

"You ready for me, baby?" he rasps.

"Always." And it's true. No matter what time of day it is, whether he's been an arse or not, I'm always ready and wanting his touch. It's like voodoo, the power he has over me. Or maybe just those magic mechanic's hands of his that know all the right places to touch.

Before I can decide, he lifts me off him, and in one fluid motion, has me bent over the back of the couch. He unbuttons my jeans and pulls them down my legs, along with my panties, leaving me bare and exposed. He kisses the back of my knee, then my thigh, trailing his tongue along the base of my arse before his teeth sink in, and I suck in a breath.

"So fucking hot." He kisses the bite mark, and the curve of my spine. His hand dips between my legs, and a whimper falls from my lips. "You want this?"

"Yes," I pant, rocking my hips against his hand.

"Yes, what?" He removes his hand, and I whimper again, mourning the loss of his touch.

"Yes, I want you inside."

I'm rewarded with a slap to my arse, but then he removes his hand again. I scowl over my shoulder.

"Stop being a tease and fuck me already."

His eyes shine with amusement as he slowly takes hold of his belt buckle and pulls it from his jeans, one loop at a time.

I spin around, landing on the couch with my legs splayed. "Take your time. I'll just do it myself." I hold his gaze as my hand slides down my body.

Matiu growls, snapping the belt out quickly and tossing it aside before dropping his jeans to the floor. He takes hold of my wrist, staying my hand, and yanks me to my feet.

"That's more like it." I grin, swiping my tongue across his lips.

He palms my arse, lifting me and wrapping my legs around him simultaneously. His hot length presses against my entrance, but it's not enough. I need more.

"Soon, baby." He pushes my back up against the wall, and before I can catch my breath, he pushes inside. I lean my head back with a groan, but he catches my lips, stifling any sound.

We move together in a frenzy, my hands clawing at his back, and his gripping my arse. It builds slowly, that warmth that begins in the pit of my stomach and spreads throughout until every nerve ending is on fire.

"I'm… I'm…" My head falls back, my mouth open in a silent scream of pleasure as he takes me over the edge. I can't move, can't think, I just hang on for dear life as he thrusts deeper, chasing his own release.

"Fuck!" He stills, pushed to the hilt, his cock throbbing inside. Our lips meet, then our foreheads, as we pant, coming down from our high.

"God I needed that," he says, easing my legs from around his waist.

"You're welcome." I grin, giving him a gentle shove as I slip past him and head towards the bathroom to clean up. "Oh, by the way, I won't be home next weekend," I toss over my shoulder as I close the door. "The girls and I are going to Hanmer."

"Shiiit, woman, I see how it is. Butter me up with sex then drop a bomb on me."

I wait for him to realise what this means.

"Aw hell no."

There it is.

"You are not leaving me to look after your dad while you go away."

I poke my head out the door to see him standing with his arms folded and a cigarette between his lips. He's still in all his naked glory, and I can't help but look him up and down with appreciation.

"Oh no you don't. My eyes are up here, woman."

"Just checking out the merchandise." I waggle my brows at him, but he doesn't stop scowling. Letting out a sigh, I cup a hand to his cheek. "I'll see if Mum can talk to him."

He snorts. "I'm sure that'll go down well."

36

My parents are in the process of separating. My mother, who doesn't approve of my choices, kicked my father out just over a month ago. No explanation.

Understandably, he isn't taking it so well. She and I were his whole life. He'd been looking forward to coming to stay for the weekend, having some father-daughter time, and getting to know Matiu better. They've lived very different lives and have absolutely nothing in common, but Dad has been looking forward to bonding with his soon-to-be son-in-law. Secretly, I think he's hoping Matiu will be like the son he never had. Having a potty-mouthed, sarcastic daughter who isn't girly in the slightest isn't quite the same.

"On second thoughts, maybe I'll leave Mum out of it and just call him tomorrow. Maybe we can change it to this weekend instead." I grin, swiping the cigarette from his hand and placing it between my lips, knowing he won't be happy about this option either.

"Oh, great. I'll just get him to tag along with me and Stubbs when we sort this knob-end out for Jeri." He rolls his eyes, snatching the cigarette back. "That'll go down *real* well."

"If you're gonna be a pussy about it, I'll just tell him not to come." I scowl up at him, my arms folded across my chest.

"Shiiit." He scrubs a hand through his hair. "Don't be like that, woman. You know I'll do it." With a finger beneath my chin, he tilts my head up, kissing the tip of my nose. "Don't know what we'll talk about though."

37

"Thank you." I push up on my toes and wrap my arms around his neck, kissing him. "I'm sure you can find *something* to talk about with him."

Yeah, right.

CHAPTER FIVE

MATEO

Stubbs and Cassian are already waiting when I pull into the lot. Loverboy is sporting another hickey on his neck, this one an even deeper red. Whoever he's hooking up with sure likes to make her claim known. By the shit-eating grin on his face, Cassian's clearly not bothered by it. Hell, he's wearing it like a goddamn badge of honour. I chuckle, pulling my helmet from my head. Good for him, I suppose.

"What's the plan?" I ask, lighting a cigarette and taking a deep drag. There's something about nicotine right after a ride. It hits different.

"According to Zeb, Curtis'll be heading to Maggie Mae's for a feed about now. I don't know about you, but I'm feeling a bit hungry." Stubbs offers a gap-toothed grin, the toothpick he's been flicking side-to-side held between his front teeth.

"I could eat," Cassian adds. I don't know where he puts it. The guy's as thin as a fucking stick, but he can pack away the food like nobody's business.

"Lead the way." I toss my cigarette butt to the ground and stamp it out.

Stubbs climbs onto his cruiser and revs the engine. With a nod of his head, he kicks up the stand and pulls out and down the long drive to the road. We cruise in a line, heading to the outskirts of town where Maggie Mae's Diner is. She's a staple ingredient to Brookhaven, and anyone coming to or from town makes a stop there. Made out of an old shipping container and painted a pale pink, she stands out against the greenery around her, drawing people in.

We pull into the already packed parking lot. No matter what time of day, Maggie Mae's is always booming. Best burgers in town, or even the country, in my opinion. Once you've had one of her famous Brookhaven Beasts, you won't ever buy a burger anywhere else. Best damn thing you can put in your mouth.

Well… I think back to last night and Barb's taste on my tongue. Maybe the second best.

"You ready?" Stubbs slaps a hand on my shoulder, and I nod.

"Lead the way."

Cassian is damn near bouncing on his toes. There's a light in his eyes, like a kid on Christmas morning. I get it. He's never been involved in any of our past scuffles, and it's exciting the first time. Adrenalin kicks in, and you're ready to take on anyone. But he also hasn't had to deal with the aftermath of when things go wrong. All it takes is one muppet to try and play the hero and then it's every man for himself.

Stubbs leads the way, pushing through the double doors and giving a nod to Clara behind the counter. She busies herself drying dishes, all the while following us with her eyes. We've never stirred shit in here before, but there's something about the leathers and patches that puts people on edge.

In the very back corner, stuffing his face with bacon, eggs and hashbrowns, sits Curtis. He's so intent on his food, he doesn't even notice us until Stubbs and Cassian have slid into the booth. I remain standing, my arms folded across my chest as I block his way out.

"Hello, Curtis," Stubbs says, clasping his hands on the table in front of him.

Curtis tosses his cutlery onto the table, grabbing a napkin and wiping his mouth slowly. He leans back, one arm slung over the back of the chair. "What's this all about then?" He glances at each of us, a surly look on his face. "You the welcoming committee?"

Stubbs snorts, reaching forward to swipe a rasher of bacon from the plate and shove it in his mouth. He shakes his head as he chews. "You know who we are."

Curtis runs his tongue along his front teeth. "Am I meant to be scared?" He leans across the table,

41

flicking a finger across the Hellhounds insignia on Cassian's vest. Cass scowls and bats his hand away. I lean in closer.

"Don't fucking touch."

Curtis holds both hands up, grinning. "Bitchy. Must be your time of the month, huh?"

"Cut the crap," Stubbs snarls before I can get a word in. "We know what you're about, and we don't want any of your shit in our town, right?"

Curtis puts on a high-pitched voice. "We don't want any of your shit in our town," he mimics. "Far as I can see, you don't own this place. Just because you're pissing everywhere and marking your territory, don't mean it's yours." He leans in. "And between you and me, I was invited." He sits back against the seat, a smug look on his face.

"Invited by who?"

"Pope Francis, who do ya think?" He rolls his eyes. "You might not like what 'crap' I do, but your mayor certainly does."

"He's fucking lying," I say, folding my arms across my chest. "No way Juanita invited him here."

Curtis cocks his head. "Believe what you want." He tips the last of his coffee back then pushes up from the table. "If we're done here, I have somewhere to be." He pushes past me, and I stare after him, unsure if I should follow or not. I don't believe for a second that Juanita would have anything to do with this guy. She's as down to earth as they come. She and Ma go way back. They've been friends forever, and I've never known her to be anything but straight up. She came to every one of my school events as a kid and was a volunteer firefighter for ten years. You don't lead that kind of life then start drug running, or worse. Not with her history.

"Let him go," Stubbs says. "We'll report back to Jeri and see what he says."

"You can't think Juanita is in on this. There is no way she's crooked. No fucking way."

"I'm not saying she is." He groans as he stands, waiting for Cassian to move out of the booth. "But it wouldn't hurt to look into it."

"So that's it then?" Cassian asks, his eyes darting back and forth between us. "Just a chat and we let him walk away?"

Slapping a hand on his shoulder, I guide him towards the door. "I hate to break it to ya, kid, but it was never gonna be a brawl."

"I know, I just thought it'd be more…" He waves his hand in the air like he's trying to find the word. "Just more."

I snicker. "You joined the wrong club, man."

He shakes his head. "It's not the wrong club. Plenty goes on. You torched a place and had a gun fight with a gangster. Why can't I get in on that action?"

Sometimes I forget how new to this he is, how like him I had been in the early days. Torching that place was an adrenalin rush, for sure, but we never meant to hurt anyone. And the gun fight… We lost a great man that night. It's not something I'd want to go through again, and I certainly wouldn't want him to be part of it either.

"It might sound like a good time, but it ain't. Believe me. You don't wanna get caught up in that kinda shit, man."

"Matiu's right. We've done some stupid shit over the years, and every time, we've lost a part of ourselves. Physically," he holds up the hand missing a finger, "mentally," he taps the side of his head, "and a damn sight more." His voice breaks as he thumps a hand to his chest. "You don't want to see your best friend with a bullet to the head."

Cassian ducks his head. He hadn't been with us long when Tony was killed, but the shock of it affected us all. "Sorry," he mumbles. "I didn't think."

"That's nothing new." I grin, slapping a hand to his chest.

Cassian snort-laughs, punching me in the shoulder. "Shut up, dick."

"Strong comeback, man. You really hurt my feelings." I clutch a hand to my chest.

"Jesus Christ, you two." Stubbs shakes his head, but he's laughing. "I can't take you anywhere."

CHAPTER SIX

BARB

"Pumpkin." Dad saunters towards me, his arms spread wide.

"Hey, Dad." I smile, falling into his embrace. It doesn't matter how old I am, there's nothing quite like being in the arms of my father.

"You're looking good. All set for the big day?" He holds me at arm's length, looking me up and down.

"I'd bloody better be. Too late to change anything now." I grin.

"It's never too late." He gives me a pointed stare, and I roll my eyes.

"Don't you start too. I've already had this conversation with Mum. I'm not going to change my mind."

He holds his hands up. "I didn't mean that, pumpkin. I know he's your 'bae'." He grins, and I snort out a laugh.

"You did *not* just say that."

"Did I use it wrong?" He runs a hand through his shaggy hair. "The kids at school told me it meant before all else. Did they catfish me?"

I shake my head. "That's not what catfishing is, Dad. But you did use it right, it's just weird hearing *you* say it."

"What? I'm hip. I'm with it." He does a little jig, ending with jazz hands, and I swear, I die a little inside. How did this wholesome, down-to-earth guy create me? More to the point, what the hell did he ever see in my drunk of a mother?

"*Sooooo* cool," I deadpan, grabbing his arm and dragging him inside before the neighbours can see. "I'm sure the kids agree."

"My cupboards aren't full of 'world's best teacher' mugs for no reason. They love me." He puffs out his chest and grabs hold of his cardigan, like you would a pair of suspenders. My father, the nerdy professor.

He follows me through to the kitchen where I flick the jug on. "Coffee?"

"Does a cow say moo?"

I turn to the cupboard and pull down two mugs, smiling my arse off. I forgot how cheesy he can be. I really should make more of an effort to spend time with him. Especially now with Mum walking out.

"This is a lovely place." He pokes his head through to the living area, whistling through his teeth. "Those classic cars are something, aren't they?" He hooks a thumb over his shoulder in the direction of the back wall. "I always wanted one of these." He points to an Impala Matiu helped Aldrin fix up last year.

"Yeah, they're pretty nice. One of the old guys from the classic car club brings them into the garage all the time. Matiu services them and sometimes gives him a hand with rebuilds."

"So none of them are yours then?"

"Matiu wishes. From what he tells me, they're a little out of our price range."

Dad nods, joining me at the counter. "They are pricey, but what an investment." He stares into his mug. "I always wanted to have a project car, something I could tinker with in the weekends."

"I didn't know that. Why didn't you then?"

He laughs. "Your mother wouldn't let me. She said I didn't know what I was doing and would just mess up the garage. Truth be told, I don't know the first thing about engines, so she was right. I would've been out of my depth." He gives me a wistful look. "She always knew me better than I knew myself."

I cluck my tongue against the roof of my mouth. "Pfft, you're a teacher. You had to study your arse off to become one. If anyone can learn how to fix up an engine, it's you."

He smiles, patting my hand. "Still some life in this old dog, you reckon?"

"Plenty." I glance at the clock. "Maybe Matiu could take you to the garage when he gets back. Show you around. Maybe teach you a thing or two for when you get your own project car."

Dad's eyes light up. "Now that would be a treat. Where is he anyway?" He turns to look over his shoulder.

"He had a job to do. Club business. He should be back soon." He'd better be anyway.

"Club business." He nods his head, tapping a finger to the side of his nose. "Understood. It all sounds very clandestine, doesn't it?"

My mouthful of coffee goes down the wrong way when I snort, and I bark out a cough, slapping a hand to my chest. "Only you would think something like that. He's not a spy, Dad." The idea of Matiu trying to be covert and discrete is laughable. He's like a toddler on Christmas day at the best of times.

"I know, I know. But it all seems so exciting to me. Riding motorcycles, protecting the town, getting your hands dirty." He looks down at his own hands, smooth and soft. "The closest these hands have come to being dirty was in the birthing suite when you were born."

I curl my lip in disgust. "Ewww. I don't want to know."

"Aww, come on, it's one of my favourite stories." He wraps an arm around my shoulders. "Your mother had been in labour for hours, and you'd just started crowning. In and out, in and out."

I dry wretch at the mental image that produces.

"Your wee head popped out, but you were in distress. The cord was wrapped around your neck."

I nod. I know the story well, but it doesn't stop him repeating it every chance he gets.

"The midwife untangled you, but then you got stuck. One of the nurses helped hold your mother up, while I climbed into the tub with her. The midwife told me to be ready to catch you as she got you loose." He sniffles, dabbing at his eye. "You were the most beautiful thing I'd ever seen. Still are."

I've heard this story a million times, but this is the first time it's brought tears to my eyes. I blink them away. I don't know what's gotten into me lately. First the wedding dress fitting, now this. I don't do emotions. Not the wishy-washy kind anyway. Jealousy, yes. Anger, definitely. But whatever this is? Nope.

A familiar rumbling comes from outside, getting louder as it draws near. Dad sits up straight, sniffing away his tears. He takes hold of his mug, then lets it go, dropping his hands by his side, then stands and sits back down.

I place my hand over his. "Chill, Dad."

The front door swings open and Matiu marches in, flinging it closed behind him. "Well that went down like a pile of shit," he calls out as he makes his way through to the kitchen. "Oh, shiiit," he says under his breath when he sees my dad sitting beside me. "Hey, Mr. Parker." He holds his hand out. "You're here early." He looks to me with wide eyes, and I mouth a silent apology. I may have neglected to tell him Dad

49

was coming first thing this morning. He practically jumped in his car the minute we finished our call.

"You know what they say about the early bird," Dad says, standing to shake his hand.

Matiu quirks a brow.

Dad's shoulders sag. "It catches the worm?" His voice goes up at the end, like he's asking a question.

"Oh, right." Matiu gives a half-hearted laugh.

"Ah… Barb tells me you've been out on secret club business." He winks in an overexaggerated way.

I wince, rubbing a finger and thumb across my temples. This is not going well.

"Ah…" Matiu's eyes flick between my father and me.

"It's okay, I don't expect you to tell me what you've been doing. I know the drill. You'd have to kill me if you told me, right?" Dad chuckles, nudging Matiu with his elbow.

"Sure." Matiu draws the word out, looking to me for help.

"It's not that kind of club, Dad."

"Oh, I know. I was just joshing with you." He nudges him again before clearing his throat and clapping his hands. "So…."

I jump in. "Dad was hoping you could show him around the garage."

Matiu's eyes widen, and he gives me what can only be described as a death stare. I give him one back, mouthing the words, 'you promised'.

With a long sigh, he rakes his hand through his hair. "Yeah, sure. Anything for you, *darling*." He lays it on thick, and he'll pay for it later, but right now, I'm just happy to see the smile on my dad's face.

CHAPTER SEVEN

MATIU

If standing here in Lawson's Lugs with Marty Parker doesn't prove my love for Barb, I don't know what does. He means the world to her, I get it, but he tries way too hard.

"So this is where the magic happens, huh?" He stands with hands on hips as his eyes flit about the place.

"I guess you could say that." I point out the pit and the four-post lift; neither of which are very impressive without a car on them. I unlock the next roller door and heft it upwards to reveal the latest in Aldrin's collection.

Marty's jaw drops and he looks like he's about to cream his pants. I can't say I blame him. "Is that…?" He stumbles forward, his hand outstretched as if to stroke the black and white beauty, but not quite making connection.

"1957 Chevy Bel Air," I say, tapping the bonnet. "Sexy, right?"

"You can say that again." He walks around her slowly, his eyes lit up. "My grandfather had one of these when I was growing up."

"No shit?"

"Wasn't quite as nice as this one, but it was beautiful all the same." He bends down to look through the window. "I always hoped I'd get it when he was gone."

"What happened?" I ask, and I'm genuinely interested in hearing the answer. Barb's said he was car mad, but I thought she was just blowing smoke up my arse, trying to get me to like him.

"My father sold it to pay off the mortgage. We already had a car, so…" He trails off, but it's obvious he's still gutted about it. "Anyway. Water under the bridge, as they say." He chuckles lightly, but I can tell it's not real. The water is stuck behind a damn and not flowing anywhere near the damn bridge from where I'm standing. Shit, to have something so precious ripped out from underneath you like that… pure torture.

"That's rough, man, I'm sorry."

He nods, slapping a hand on my shoulder as he walks past, giving the car the respect it deserves in a slow walk around. "She really is beautiful."

"Aldrin knows his shit. You should check out his collection while you're out here."

"That would be amazing."

"I'll give him a call. See if we can't jack something up." I eye him, then glance up at the clock on the wall. Two fifteen in the afternoon. Is it too early to suggest a drink? I know I could use one, and after his emotional trip down memory lane, I'm sure he could too.

"You know what? Why don't I show you the bar?" Without waiting for his response, I march towards the office and the hall alongside it.

"There's a bar here?" Marty falls into step beside me, shaking his head. "Certainly makes after work drinks easy."

I chuckle. "You have no idea. Jeri lives upstairs." I point to the stairs at the far end. "We've all crashed there at some point." Some of us more than others, but that was before I had a woman keeping my bed warm at night. "Still can't figure out how we make it up those damn stairs though. Bloody things are a death trap when you're sober, but somehow we manage when we're blind drunk." I laugh again, nudging him with my elbow before thinking better of it.

"Sounds like a riot. Our work drinks are much tamer in comparison." He shoves his hands in his pockets, rocking back on his heels. "A few vinos at the local establishment and then everyone heads off their separate ways."

I push through the door, holding it open for him. His eyes take in every inch of the place in a matter of seconds, then he lets out a low whistle. "Wow."

I try to see it through his eyes. I'm so used to the dimly lit room with bar leaners dotted about the place and a makeshift bar made out of an old plane wing balanced on a couple of drums wrapped in corrugated iron. I guess it has its charm. Rustic, I think.

"What'll you have?" I ask, slipping in behind the bar and almost arsing over as the back of my heels hit something solid that groans. "What the fuck?" I turn to find Cassian staring up at me from the floor. "The fuck are you doing?"

He swipes a hand down his face, curling on his side, his back to me. "Must've fallen asleep." He shrugs, climbing to his feet. The fucker won't even look at me. He brings his hand up to scratch the back of his neck, busying himself behind the bar.

"Seemed plenty awake at the diner this morning," I press. "Something happen, kid?" Taking hold of his shoulder, I swing him round to face me. Cassian's eye is black and swollen shut, his top lip split and bleeding. Anger boils in the pit of my belly. "Jesus. Who the fuck did this to you?"

"No one." He juts his chin up. "Doesn't matter."

"The fuck it doesn't." I tilt his head back to get a better look. "That's some fucking shiner for a Mr. Nobody."

Marty clears his throat, reminding me of his presence, and here I am, swearing my fucking arse off in front of him. Barb's going to kill me. "Mind if I take

55

a look?" He holds his hands up, palms out. "I'm one of the first-aiders at work."

"Be my guest." I step back, still fuming. Jeri's not going to be happy about one of our own being attacked.

"Ah, hi, I'm Marty. Barbara's dad." He holds his hand out to Cassian before realising he can't see it. "I'm just going to touch your face." He rubs his palms together, warming them before holding them up and gently probing around Cassian's jaw and cheekbones. Cass hisses.

Marty lets out a slow sigh. "I'm afraid you may have a fracture. Best to get to a doctor and have them check it out, I think." He brushes his hands on his pants. "Whoever did this must've had one heck of a right hook."

"This related to our meetup this morning?" I ask, and Cass shakes his head, wincing.

"Nah, nothing to do with it."

"You sure?" I level his good eye with a stare. "You better not be shitting with me."

"Honest, bro, it wasn't them."

I search his eyes until I'm convinced. Nodding, I allow myself to relax some. "Who was it then?"

Cassian tilts his head back, letting out a groan. "You're gonna think I'm stupid."

"Too late for that, kid." I chuckle, and he flips me the bird.

"Fucker."

A thought occurs to me, and I can't help but grin. "Oh shiiiiit, this was your lady friend, wasn't it?" He doesn't deny it, just ducks his head, and I throw my head back, laughing. "Oh, mate, you are never gonna live this one down. What'd you do?"

"It's not like that, man," he says, swiping a bag of ice from the freezer and holding it to his eye.

"Sure it isn't."

"It wasn't her, okay? But it was to do with her." He stares down at the bar.

"Oh, bro, you didn't?"

"I didn't know she had a guy already." He shrugs.

"Shiiiit, man, that's such a rookie mistake. You *always* do your homework, right, Marty?"

"Oh yes." He nods his head fervently. "Can't be cutting another man's lunch."

Cassian screws up his nose. "Huh?"

"He means you don't go shagging someone else's Mrs. Bros before hoes, am I right?" I jostle Marty with my elbow before realising how bad that probably sounded. "I mean, not that all ladies are hoes or anything." I reach up and grip the back of my neck. "Barb's definitely not, and she comes before anyone else."

Cassian snorts out a laugh, and my eyes widen as I groan. "Fuck, you know what I mean." Goddamn it. Stupid mouth running away on me again.

"I do, and I appreciate that you're looking after her. She means the world to me, that girl." Marty pats his hand on my shoulder. If it were any other guy doing and saying that, I'd take it as a threat, but with Marty, it's the honest truth. I can see it in his eyes.

"I'll always look after her, you don't have to worry about that." I know I'm punching well above my weight with Barb. There's no way I'd do anything to fuck it up. Sure, I was a dick who didn't fully appreciate her in the beginning, but after she came storming through the bushes with me to save Sam, something changed. For the first time there was a real possibility I could lose her, and the thought terrified me. I ain't never going to feel that way again. I turn back to Cass. "You really like her, huh?" He has to to let this happen.

He nods. "I do."

"You better make goddamn sure she's worth all this trouble."

"She is."

I lean in. "You get a few punches in?"

He grins. "I held my own."

"Good shit, bro."

CHAPTER EIGHT

BARB

When I sent Dad and Matiu off together, I didn't expect them to be gone the rest of the afternoon. I also didn't expect them to come home in high spirits, reeking of booze, acting like old pals. Don't get me wrong, I want them to get along, but seeing them all buddy-buddy is surreal. It's like I've stepped into an episode of *The Twilight Zone.*

"I don't know who he's got himself caught up with, but Cass is in for a world of hurtin' if he keeps shacking up with this bird." Matiu laughs, tearing a bread roll in half before slathering it with butter. "You should've seen the work they did on his face."

"It certainly wasn't pretty," Dad adds. "A fracture, at the very least. Poor lad." He shakes his head.

"At least he gave it back as good as he got. Still, not a great way to start a relationship," I say, carving into the roast lamb on my plate.

"The heart wants what the heart wants," Dad offers up. "Even if it's a preposterous idea." He shakes his head. "Oh to be young and naïve again."

"Jesus," Barb says. "He's dumber than I thought then."

"Now, pumpkin, you have to remember he's just a baby. Romance is new to him."

Matiu snorts. "I don't think it's romance he's after there, Marty." He pumps his fist back and forth in line with his mouth, his tongue protruding through his cheek. I level him with a stare, slapping his arm with the back of my hand.

Dad chuckles. "No, I suppose you're probably right there."

My knife and fork clatter onto my plate, and I tilt my head skywards, inhaling deeply. I expect this sort of shit from Matiu, but now my father's in on it? It's all kinds of wrong. "What did you do to my father?"

They both laugh, and Dad pats my hand in what I assume is meant to be a soothing manner, but it just irritates me. I slide it out from under his touch and point an accusatory finger at Matiu. "You're a bad influence."

He holds his hands up, palms out. "Hey, you wanted this, remember?" He gestures between the two

60

of them. "You sent us off to the garage together knowing your dad is a freakin' car nut, by the way. What'd you think was gonna happen? Shiiiit, woman."

He's right, I suppose. I have no one to blame but myself. But really, how was I supposed to anticipate this? Under normal circumstances, they'd never get on. They're too different. One sweet and innocent, the other rough as guts. But throw in a hot rod and a fist fight, and I guess they're all the same.

Still, as much as I want them to like each other, it's weird to see my dad laughing along to Matiu's depraved sense of humour. It's... gross. He's my strait-laced dad who teaches high schoolers about science. He's not a locker-room-talk kind of guy. At least, I didn't think he was.

"So, I guess now isn't a good time to tell you I invited your pops to my stag do then?" Matiu grins at me, tossing a wink in Dad's direction.

I snort. "Okay."

"I would very much like to go."

"Seriously?" I can't picture it. My dad amongst the Hellhounds, getting on the turps. It's laughable. There's no way he'll enjoy himself.

He clears his throat. "Seriously. That is to say, if you're okay with it, pumpkin," he says with a note of optimism in his voice.

I screw my nose up, not liking where this is headed one bit, but considering I threw the two of them together, I can hardly complain now, can I? "Ugh, fine, whatever." I wave my hand through the air. "It's clear something went down at the garage today, and I'm not gonna break up this…" I flick my finger between the two of them, grimacing. "Whatever *this* is."

Dad's face lights up. "Wonderful."

"At least I can count on you to make sure he doesn't get too shitfaced." I point my knife at Matiu, then bark out a laugh. "Who am I kidding? Nothing could stop that from happening. Right, babe?"

He clutches his hand to his chest, like he always does when I give him shit. Like he did that first time we met a few years ago. "Shiiiit, woman, you wound me."

"Harden up." I grin, and he returns it.

"It's always hard for you, baby."

Dad clears his throat, blotting a napkin to his face before tossing it on his plate. "I think that's my cue to vacate the room."

Matiu has the decency to look embarrassed, but only just. It takes a lot to shake him. "Sorry, Marty."

"No, no, I understand. Young love and all that. Not that any father wants to envisage his daughter doing… that…" He clears his throat again, rubbing at his chin and avoiding my eyes. "Anyway, I best be off. Long drive back."

"You sure you won't stay the night? I made up the spare room," I offer.

"Yeah, don't leave on my account. I'll keep it strictly PG from now on, I swear." Matiu crosses a finger over his heart and holds his hand up like he's about to swear on a bible.

"I wouldn't want to impose…" His voice trails off, but he doesn't move to leave. Ever since Mum walked out, he's been so lonely. So despondent. And as much as I hate to admit it, it's been good for him to hang out with Matiu and loosen up a little. Don't get me wrong, it's still weirding me out, this odd camaraderie they seem to have formed over Cassian getting beat up, but whatever. If it eases Dad's loneliness, then I can let them have their fun.

"Please stay, Dad."

"I…" He searches my eyes, for what, I don't know, but whatever it is, he seems to find it. His shoulders lower from around his neck and he smiles. "Okay then. If you're sure?"

"Of course we're sure, old man. Sit your arse back down." Matiu kicks out the seat from under the table, and I shoot him a warning glare.

Dad just laughs, joining us once more. "Easy on the old man, son. There's still some life in me yet."

"Believe it or not, 'old man' is a term of endearment in Matiu's eyes. Reserved for only the staunchest of men." He's called Jericho 'old man' for as long as I've known him, and Jeri's only a few years his senior. Matiu likes to be the jokester, but really, he has nothing but respect for Jericho.

Dad's chest puffs out, and he pretends to dust something off his shoulder. "Well, I shall wear that name as a badge of honour then. Thank you." He nods his head in gratitude, and it's hard to hide the smile forming on my lips. My dad has always been a bit of a dork, but damn I love him.

Hellhounds MC

CHAPTER NINE

MATU

"Are you sure your mother won't mind me stopping by unannounced like this?" Marty asks as we walk up the path. He keeps tugging at his cardigan like a nervous teenager. Fuck knows why. Ma loves Barb, so it goes without saying she'll fall head over heels for her dad. I mean, the guy's a bit of a nerd, but he's full of heart, and he raised one hell of a daughter.

I slap a hand on his shoulder. "Positive. Just don't wear your shoes inside and you'll be sweet as."

Barb snickers beside me, and I nudge her with my elbow. Just because she can do no wrong in the eyes of Ma, doesn't mean we all get the same treatment. Shit, I grew up with her, and I don't get treated half as good as Barb, or Holden for that matter. Ma and her goddamn favourites.

The door swings open before we even make it up the steps and Ma throws her arms out wide. "My girl!" She beckons Barb to her, pulling her in for a hug and a kiss to the cheek. She peeks over Barb's shoulder, taking in the ball of nerves behind me. "And who do we have here?" As she steps back from Barb's embrace, she reaches up and pats at her hair like she's trying to tame it, tucking strands behind her ears.

"Mama K, my dad, Marty. Dad, Mama K." Barb points between the two of them, not that Ma seems to be paying much attention. Her eyes are riveted to Marty, and it's kind of creeping me out. I know she hasn't had a man in her life for a while, but Marty? That's all kinds of wrong.

"Ah, hi." Marty waves, stepping forward. "Sorry to show up out of the blue like this. I hope we didn't catch you at an inconvenient time." He offers her his hand, and she steps forward, a confused look on her face as her eyes flick between him and Barb. I get it. Barb is the female version of Marty, only hot. Even though their personalities are polar opposites, there's no mistaking they're from the same gene pool.

"Oh of course not." She flaps her hands about as if shooing away a fly. "I was just doing some baking."

"Ah, that would be the delicious aroma coming from inside." He inhales deeply. "Something with cinnamon and apples, if I'm not mistaken?"

Ma beams. She takes her baking seriously, and anyone who shows enthusiasm for food is an instant friend. "You know your stuff. Mama K's homemade apple pie, fresh out of the oven. It should be cool enough to eat now. Would you like a slice?"

"How can I say no to such an offer?" Marty climbs the steps and shucks his shoes off, tucking them to the side. He gives her a nod then follows her through with a backward glance at us.

"We'll never get him outta there now, not after he's had a slice of her pie. That shit is legendary." I kick my own boots off and leave them where they land. I'm not about to let anyone else have my helping, even if he *is* Barb's dad.

She barks out a laugh. "Scared you're gonna miss out?" The woman is a damn mind-reader. "Unlike you, his stomach doesn't control him."

I pause on the step, turning back to her. "Shiiit, woman. You know that's not what controls me." Taking hold of her hip, I pull her in close, thrusting against her.

"Oh, you mean *I'm* what controls you?" She grins, poking her tongue between her teeth and grinding her hips.

My fingers flex, gripping her tightly as I lean into it. God, this woman will be the death of me. "That's not what I was saying at all." I suck in a breath as she rotates her hips again. "Jesus H. Christ. If you don't stop grinding yourself on me, we're gonna be putting on a show for the whole neighbourhood to see." I groan as she gives one final push against me. Then she turns on her heels, bending at the waist to undo her fuck-me boots, her perfect arse in the air. I give it a slap, my hand lingering on her softness before she straightens and without so much as a bat of the eye, heads inside. Adjusting myself, I huff out another groan before following suit.

Inside, Ma and Marty are talking up a storm. Her bench is covered with bowls and trays of cookies, and right in the centre is the apple pie. There's already a large slice missing.

"Matiu, your mother is an amazing cook. I don't know how you're not the size of a house, growing up with food this good." He shovels another piece of pie into his mouth.

I try to ignore the fact that I haven't been offered any pie yet and slap my stomach. "Guess I just have a fast metabolism. Never have to work out, never put on any weight. It's a gift."

"Must be good genes." Marty smiles at Ma. "If only the rest of us mere mortals could be so lucky. I'll have to get on the treadmill to burn this off."

"Since when do you go to the gym?" Barb asks with a snort. "Please don't tell me you're having a mid-life crisis. I'm still wrapping my head around Mum's." She winces. "Sorry, Dad."

He pats her hand. "You don't have to watch what you say around me, pumpkin. I know this has had an effect on you too. No one ever expects their parents to separate. I certainly didn't see it coming." He purses his lips, a wistful expression on his face. Shifting in his seat, he clears his throat. "And you're right, I don't go to the gym. I signed up once as a New Year's resolution, but I don't think I even stepped foot in the door." He chuckles, but his heart isn't in it.

"You got yourself an in-home gym then, Marty?" I ask, trying to keep the conversation going. The poor guy looks as though he's about to cry. Can't say I blame him. I'd be lost if Barb cut ties and walked out on me.

"Oh gosh, no. No, I only said I'd have to get on one to burn it off, not that I'm going to. My attempt at making a joke, I'm afraid." He laughs again.

"Oh!" Ma bursts out, clapping her hands. "Oh, you are a hoot. I can see where Barb gets her sense of humour from."

That lights up his eyes. "Chip off the old block, eh pumpkin?" He reaches around her shoulders and crushes her into his side. She wraps her arm around him, leaning her head on his shoulder.

"How long are you in town for, Marty?" Ma asks as she layers cookies into a tin and wipes down the bench. I can only hope that means it's nearly pie time, because damn I'm hungry.

"I head home this afternoon, then I'll be back again next weekend for this one's stag do." He hitches his thumb in my direction.

"Is that right?" Mama K looks amused, and I don't know whether to be offended or not. Sure, me and the boys like to get on it and sometimes I don't remember much of what goes down, but I'm sure Marty can hack it. He was young once.

"Yes. Looking forward to it too."

"Well, I'm sure you'll have a great time." She levels me with a stare. "And I'm sure my boy will look after you, won't you, son?"

Jesus, what's with these women and expecting me to watch over a grown-arse man? "I think Marty can hold his own."

"Absolutely. If anything, I think it's likely I'll be the one looking after Matiu here. He is the man of honour after all."

"Damn straight." I can feel Ma's eyes boring into my skull, but I don't dare look at her. Instead, I slide the plate of pie to me and take matters into my own hands. Clearly she's not going to offer me any.

"To be honest, it's probably Cassian who will need looking after," Barb says. "If he's as lovestruck as you say he is, he'll be pining all night."

"Ah yes, our young Cassanova." Marty grins. "The poor lad has it bad, I'm afraid."

"Well, Marty, looks like we'll have to show him he can still have a good time with his brothers, won't we?"

Marty sits up straighter, puffing out his chest, a goofy grin on his face. "I like that. One of the brothers."

CHAPTER TEN

BARB

I pull up outside the Alpine villa halfway up Conical Hill. A wooden balcony runs around the perimeter of the upstairs, giving a view of the sleepy town and its surrounds, while the lower half is something out of a fairytale. The front door is framed by two pillars and stained-glass panels on either side. Large windows run around the lefthand corner where it looks to be the kitchen, and a bay window juts out on the other side of the attached garage. I can see the others already inside, bustling about with their bags, and bottles of booze already line one of the tables. This weekend is going to be a good one.

The front door swings open and my mother flings her arms in the air. "Darling!" she cries, almost stumbling through the door and onto the landing. Great. She's off her face before the weekend has even begun. I'm not normally one to begrudge someone a drink or a good time, but this is taking the piss. Every damn time I've seen her lately she's been enjoying a drink or four. You'd think she was drowning her sorrows over the separation if it wasn't for the fact she was the instigator.

I inhale deeply then huff it out, forcing myself out of the car to face it head on. "Mum, hi." I slam the car door then stomp around to the boot to retrieve my bag.

"I hope you don't mind, I started without you." She holds up a half-filled champagne flute. "Thought I'd better do some quality control. This one passes muster."

Good, because I'm going to need a large one of those, immediately.

"That's *great*, Mum."

If she picks up on the sarcasm dripping from my voice, she doesn't react. "Come, come, come." She waves her hand, ushering me inside. "Let's get you a drink."

"Mmhmm," I mumble, pushing past her. Sam saunters my way, grabbing my bag from me.

"I'll show you to your room." She glances over my shoulder then whispers, "I tried to stop her."

I don't know whether to laugh or cry at that statement. It's bad enough that *I* can see she has a problem, but for my friends to pick up on it too? That's a whole new low I wasn't wanting to stoop to this weekend.

"It's okay. I don't think a steamroller could've stopped her from getting her mouth wrapped around one of those drinks." I shrug to play it off as nothing, but the look in Sam's eyes says she's not buying it. I guess when you have a shitty parent, you learn to recognise it in others. Not that Mum ever tried to sell me off to pay a debt like her father did, or anything half as bad as that, I guess. She's just a wino going through a midlife crisis and sleeping her way around town like she's Snow fucking White. There was Dr. Jonasson, then that halfwit who flunked out of high school, in *my year*, no less. There was Alistair, the barber with an anger management problem who wound up in court after snipping off the tip of a guy's ear. And who can forget Mr. Rollins, the guy allergic to everything. So that means all she needs to complete the set is Sleepy, Happy, and Bashful. Who knows, maybe she'll strike it lucky and hit all three while she's here.

God I need a cigarette. And a drink. In that order.

After saying hello to everyone, I slip outside for some 'fresh air'. The first puff goes down smoothly, and the tension in my neck loosens. I'm here to have a good time with the girls. One last blow out before the big day. I refuse to let my mother stand in the way of that.

The door slides open behind me, and a burst of raucous laughter assaults my eardrums. "Want some company?" Sam pulls up a seat beside me, resting her feet on the banister.

"Looks like I don't have much choice in the matter," I say dryly, but really, I'm happy for the distraction.

"Damn right you don't. I hate to break it to you, Barb, but this is your hens do. You're not meant to be sitting on your own like Nellie no mates. You have to enjoy yourself." She holds her hands up as if to stop me. "I know that's hard for you to do, but it's in the rule book." She nods matter-of-factly, and I can't help but grin.

"That's rich, coming from the woman who shut herself away from the world for months." I quirk a brow at her, and she rolls her hand in front of her.

"Touche."

We sit in silence for a beat before she nudges me with her elbow. "It's just a bit of fun. She's not hurting anyone."

"Yet," I mutter under my breath.

"Well, Jen's in there keeping her company, and Darcy just brought out a huge platter of food, so that should soak up some of it." She shrugs. "Maybe she needs to let off some steam?"

I snort, taking one last drag before stubbing my cigarette in the ashtray. "That's all she's been doing for the past six weeks. Trust me, she's let off more than her share of steam."

"Yikes." Sam pulls a face like she's bitten into something bad. "I'm sorry."

I shrug. "It is what it is. Not like I can do anything about it." I peer through the window at my mother shimmying with her eyes closed. There isn't even any music playing, but there she is, dancing to her own beat.

"All the more reason to come back inside and have some fun then, right? Take your mind off it." She stands, holding her hands out to me. "You never know, you might actually enjoy yourself." She waggles her brows, pulling me to my feet.

The door slides open again, and with her hand on my lower back, she unceremoniously pushes me inside. Mum is opening another bottle of champers while dancing around the lounge to the music in her head. Jen is standing with an array of remotes in her hand, pushing buttons and holding them up to different corners of the room. When nothing happens, she tuts then moves onto the next one. There's a whirring sound and a clang out the front of the house.

"You good, Jen?" I ask, accepting the bottle of cider Sam's thrust into my hand.

"One of these must work the music, right, chickadee?" She waves them in the air. From the look of it, one is for the heat pump, another for the TV, and one looks like the garage door opener. That explains the noise. "Can't have a party without music."

"Right," Sam says, taking the remotes from her. "But you won't get any out of these, I'm afraid." She tosses them onto the coffee table and retrieves a small one from her back pocket. There's a series of beeps as she pairs her phone to the sound system, and then the familiar notes of Dave Dobbyn's *Slice of Heaven* come through the speakers.

"Yes!" Jen cries out, her hands raised to the ceiling. "This feels more like a party." She grabs my hand and drags me into the centre of the room, shaking her hips. "See this?" She gestures to her inhumanly rotating hips. "This is called dancing. You might not know it because you're too cool for school, but this is how us old folks have a good time, right, Sandra?" She grins, waggling her brows at Mum, who is so mortified she's stopped dancing.

"Who're you calling old?"

Jen chuckles, tipping her glass to Mum. "Sorry to lump you in with this old duck, Sandra. You're only as old as you feel, right?"

Mum seems to contemplate that before her lips pull back into a wide smile and her eyes glaze over. "I like you, Jen. I wasn't sure at first, but you understand me." Her eyes swivel to me, and the meaning is clear; *unlike me.*

To her credit, Jen lets the backhanded compliment slide and clinks her glass to Mum's. "Well thank you, chick. I like to think of myself as a people person. Goes with the job." She winks.

"She's right," Sam chimes in. "I was practically a recluse when I first moved to Brookhaven, and now look at me." She flings her arms out wide. "And I owe it all to these two women here." She smiles warmly, wrapping her fingers around mine and an arm around Jen's waist. "If anyone was going to bring me out of my shell, it was this lot."

"Aww." Jen rests her head on Sam's shoulder. "You know I love you, chicky. The place wouldn't be the same without you."

"You're welcome," I say, taking a bow, and Sam chuckles, giving my fingers a squeeze. We'd had a rough start, but she'd worn on me to the point I dove headfirst into a rescue mission with the Hellhounds after her then husband tracked her down and kidnapped her. We've been tight ever since.

Mum's eyes dart between the three of us, as if she's trying to work us out. I suppose we do make an odd team; a perky fifty-something, a recluse turned mother hen, and me, the moody bitch. But somehow, it works.

"Aww, this is sweet and all, but when does the drinking and debauchery really start?" Cami pipes up from the couch before shovelling a cracker loaded with cheese, gherkins, and hummus into her mouth. "This is good," she says around her mouthful, and Darcy smiles, her hands in her lap. Sam is the mother hen of the group, but Darcy is the only one of us who actually has children, and she doesn't get out all that much. Still gun-shy after what she went through with her psycho ex, I suppose, and I can't say I blame her. No one deserves that kind of shit. But it's about time she came out of her shell with us.

I swipe the bottle of champers from Mum's hand, much to her dismay, and pour a hefty slug into an empty glass on the table. Sliding it towards Darcy, I raise my brow. "You can relax, you know. Have a drink."

Her shoulders slump, and her cheeks flush. "Sorry, I've just never been this far from them before."

"They're in the best hands though, Darce. Mama K would never let anything happen to them." The boys have their stag do tonight, so Mama K jumped at the opportunity to babysit. She keeps hinting at how much she'd like to be a grandmother, and I keep pointing her towards Darcy's kids like they'll ward her off. I'm not ready to be a baby factory. I struggle to keep a bloody pot plant alive. To be honest, I don't even know if I want kids. They're loud and for some reason, always sticky, and I have enough on my plate with Matiu. He's like a kid and teen all rolled into one.

"That's what I said." Cami gives her a pointed look. "And Holden is right there if she needs him. You're golden." She picks the glass up and holds it out to her. "Let your hair down. It's been *forever*."

Darcy rolls her eyes, but a smile lights up her face. "Alright, fine." She takes a tentative sip, and her eyes close as she hums.

Cami claps her hands. "Oh yeah, now it's a party."

HELLHOUNDS MC

CHAPTER ELEVEN

MATIU

Holden slides a whiskey towards me. "I can't believe you found someone game enough to marry you." He shakes his head. "She's way outta your league, bro, I hope you know that."

I snort, taking a large mouthful and letting the slow burn creep down my throat. The first one always hits better than any that follow. "Of course I do. Why do you think I put a ring on it?" I tap my temple. "I ain't stupid, man."

"The jury's out on that one." Holden smirks, popping the top on his beer. "She's good for you though. It's about time you settled down."

"You're only saying that because you're all loved up with Darce and want everyone else to be the same."

He holds his hands out wide. "I don't deny it." And why would he? For as long as I can remember, he's had a boner for Darcy. Yeah, he had to play the long game with that one, but it turned out for the best. Now he has an instant family, and I honestly can't say I've ever seen him happier. Lucky fuck. Always was one to land on his feet.

But I guess that's me now too with Barb. I was an absolute tool when we first got together, and I'm not afraid to admit it. But she gets me like no other chick ever has. She puts up with my shit and gives it back just as hard. There's never a dull moment with her around, that's for sure.

"Jeri!" Holden calls out, beckoning him towards us. "You took your time. It's not like you have far to go, man." He rolls his eyes, and I snicker.

Jericho slaps him up the back of the head while giving Zeb the nod at the bar. "I had shit to do."

"Checking up on his old lady, no doubt," Holden mutters under his breath, and Jericho raises his hand again, making him wince.

"Don't act like you didn't already check in with Darce. We all know how pussy whipped you are."

I can't help but bark out a laugh at that one, because it's true. Whatever Darcy needs or wants, Holden is on the case before it's even come out of her mouth. I get it, he has lost time to make up for, but come on. You can't hand your balls over on a silver

79

platter like that. Shit, you've got to keep them on their toes sometimes.

Zeb brings over a whiskey for Jericho and another for me.

"Where's Cassian? I thought he was behind the bar tonight?" Jericho frowns, looking towards the front door.

Zeb shrugs. "No fucking idea. 's far as I was aware, he was meant to be here too."

"Probably out sucking face with that hoover he hooked up with."

I damn near choke on my drink. He *has* been showing up with a new hickey every damn day. Dude has more game than I thought, even if it's the reason his face is messed up.

"Jeri, you made it." Stubbs joins us with a tray of shots.

"Yeah, yeah, I know I'm late. I'm not apologising for checking on my girl. She hates driving around hills."

Holden makes a whipping sound and flicks his wrist. "Who's pussy whipped?" he quips, his brow quirked.

"You know what? Fuck it." Jeri holds his palms up. "I'll admit it."

"That's old news, old man, but I'll give you props for owning it." I slap him on the shoulder. "Can't say I blame you either. You struck it lucky with Sam."

"Don't I know it." He downs his drink and reaches for a shot, eyeballing me. "We doing this?" He holds it aloft, waiting for each of us to grab one. "To

Matiu, the luckiest son of a bitch who managed to convince a knockout like Barb to marry him."

"The fuck kinda toast is that?" I question, but I tip my glass back all the same. Liquid aniseed slides down my throat.

"Another round?" Stubbs asks, but he's already making his way back to the bar.

"Get Zeb one too!" Holden calls after him. "Poor bastard should be enjoying this with us."

"Yeah, he should." Jericho frowns again. "Where the fuck is Cass? He's been shirking his responsibilities a lot lately." He pulls his phone out, punching the screen a few times before holding it to his ear.

There's no need though, because the door swings open, and Cassian saunters in with his arm draped around a busty blonde teetering on stiletto heels.

Oh fuck no.

Zeb snickers behind me.

"Sorry I'm late." Cass pulls a stool out for her then makes his way around the back of the bar, oblivious to the stares.

Holden breaks the silence first. "What the fuck, man?" He slings a tea towel over his shoulder, his eyes flicking from Cass to the woman.

"What?"

"Unless she's here to strip, she can't be here, man. This is a stag do." Cass still doesn't seem to get it, so Zeb elaborates. "No chicks allowed."

Cassian's eyes widen as he turns in my direction. "Shit, is that true? I thought it was just a piss up." If it weren't the fucking devil incarnate he'd brought with

81

him, I'd probably be laughing, but as it is, I'm barely hanging on.

Jericho grabs my arm, holding me in place. "He doesn't know," he reminds me. To Cass, he says, "Yeah, kid, he's right. This is a boys only night."

"Oh fuck." He gives her a sheepish look. "Sorry, babe. I thought it'd be okay."

Babe? Goddamn, he's in deeper than I thought.

"You don't mind, do you?" He nods towards the door.

"Oh, don't worry, honeybun. I'm sure Matty won't mind little old me being here, right, Matty?" Her voice drips with smugness, and I can tell without looking at her that she's pouting. Typical fucking Jodi.

Cassian's eyes seem to bulge out of his head. He swallows, hard. "You two know each other?"

"Oh yeah," she answers. "We go waaaay back." She giggles, and the sound is like nails on a chalkboard. How did I ever find her attractive?

"Not far enough, clearly," I mutter beneath my breath.

Jericho steps in, marching towards the door. "Look, Jodes, it's nice to see you, but you can't be here, okay? You understand." He opens the door and holds it open for her. Outside, Barb's dad stands sheepishly, his hand raised as if he was about to knock. Fuck my life. This just got ten times more awkward.

"Aww, don't be like that. Can't we all just get along?" she sing-songs in that way that *used to* work on me, but now? Now it grates every last nerve.

"No, Jodi, we can't." I practically spit the words before tossing back the rest of my drink and grabbing for Holden's half-finished beer. "Marty, come have a drink," I call out, waving him in as if my ex isn't standing five feet from me, her eyes boring into the back of my head.

The sound of her heels clip clopping across the floor has my fists curling at my side. And when her fingers wrap around my shoulder, her breath in my ear, it takes everything inside me not to react. If Marty sees me blow my top, he'll never let me marry Barb. The guy's a pushover, but that girl is his world.

"Just because it's your stag do, doesn't mean we can't have some fun," she whispers. I shrug her off.

"Oooookaaaay." Holden gets to his feet. "Enough is enough, Jodi. You've had your fun, now it's time to leave." He takes hold of her arm, pulling her away from me.

"What if I strip?" she suggests, and I damn near choke on my drink. "He said I could stay if I was a stripper, right?" She points a long, manicured finger at Zeb. "I can shake what the good Lord gave me." She shimmies to prove her point.

Marty's cheeks redden as he joins me at the table, and he hooks his thumb over his shoulder. "Maybe I should…" I stop him with a shake of my head and slide a stool out for him.

"Stay."

Cassian rounds the bar. "Jodi, no." He frowns, his tone conflicted. "You're not stripping in front of my mates?" He says it like a question, like he's unsure if she's serious. He'll learn.

Jodi huffs out a sigh. "Oh fine, be a party pooper then." Holden guides her to the door still being held open by Jeri. "But you better get used to seeing me around, Matty. Cos I'm back."

Chapter Twelve

Barb

After polishing off the last of the wine and ciders, we make our way into what passes for nightlife in this sleepy tourist town. There are two places with music pumping, and a handful of restaurants open, but the rest of the streets are quiet.

We stumble into a bar tucked down an alleyway, where the music is at least from this century.

"First round's on me!" Mum calls out, waving her credit card in the air. She falls onto a bar stool, her finger held aloft, running the length of the bottles on the shelf. "That one." She slams her card down. "We're celebrating," she says to the bartender, who smiles at her. "My daughter... Hang on, where is she?" Her head swivels about until her gaze lands on me. "There she is!" She beckons me over, and I guess the drinks have done their thing because I go without question. Her arm lands across my shoulders, heavy, like she can't hold it up herself. "My daughter is getting married."

If I didn't know any better, I'd think she was proud. She's very good at playing the role of doting mother when she wants to.

"Is that right?" the bartender asks, offering me a grin. "Congratulations."

"Thanks." I yank on the t-shirt the girls made me put on before we left the house. It has a blown-up picture of Matiu on the front, and the words 'the ball and chain' underneath. "This is him." I don't know why I'm showing this stranger, as if he gives a shit, but this is the first time Mum has sounded even vaguely okay with the idea of me and Matiu, so I'm running with it.

"Oh." The guy frowns, glancing around the bar. "He's a lucky man." He holds up the vodka bottle Mum pointed to. "Is this for you then?"

I say, "No," at the same time Mum says, "Yes." I don't even like vodka. More of an Irish whiskey kind of gal.

"It's for *all* of us." She gestures to the others standing behind us. "Line 'em up..." She squints, leaning forward to read the guy's name tag. "Eddie."

He does as he's told, lining up half a dozen shot glasses and filling them to the brim. We each take one, and with a hearty, "Cheers," we knock them back. It burns on the way down, and I suck a breath in through my teeth.

"Another!" Mum says, slapping her hand on the bar. Where was this version of her when I was 18 and wanted to party all night and sleep all day?

Once again, we salute then tip them back, only this time, Jen holds her hand over the empty glasses. "That's enough for now. We want to be able to make it home in one piece." She laughs, and Mum gives her the side eye before grinning back at her.

"The night'sstill young," she slurs, circling her finger in the air. "Hold it for us, Ed." She pulls out the finger guns before Jen drags her away to a booth.

"Your mum's a riot." Cami laughs, nudging me in the ribs with her elbow.

"That's one way of putting it," I deadpan, pulling up a stool and propping myself against the bar.

"She must've been a blast to grow up with. No wonder you turned out the way you did."

I snort, almost offended at the suggestion. "Believe me, she wasn't always like…" I wave my hand in her direction, "…this. She was way more uptight and strict. I turned out like this *despite* her."

"Yeah?" I can tell she doesn't believe me.

The music changes, and her eyes light up. "I love this song! Let's dance!" She takes hold of Darcy's hand and drags her to the centre of the empty room. Darcy looks like a fish out of water, her hips jerking side-to-side to a beat all of their own, her hands hanging limp by her side. Cami is dancing circles around her, shaking her hips and waving her arms in the air. The look on Darcy's face is something akin to a deer in headlights, and I can't help but feel sorry for her.

Sam chuckles beside me. "I think I'll go rescue her." She shimmies her way over, taking hold of Darcy's hands and joining in the dance. I don't know that I'd class it as rescuing her, but Darcy at least looks a little less like she's going to shit herself. There's even the makings of a smile on her face.

A short, stocky Māori guy steps into my field of view, his eyes homed in on my chest. "Ahh, why've you got Anaru's face on your top?"

I fold my arms. "Eyes are up here, buddy."

He shakes his head then meets my gaze with a lopsided grin. "Oh nah, I wasn't checkin' you out or anything. Just…" he points to my chest, "why is Anaru's face on your top, and why does it look like you're getting hitched to him?" He scratches his head, a frown wrinkling his brow. "Shazza will have a thing or two to say about that." He snorts.

"Ah, I don't know who *Anaru* is, but this is my fiancé, Matiu." I tug the hem of my top out, pointing at his face.

The guy leans in closer until I cough, giving him a pointed look. "Sorry." He laughs, holding his hands up. "Looks so much like him." His gaze seems to travel over me more closely. "You're waaaaaay outta his league though, and young enough to be his daughter." He snickers, taking a swig of his beer. "Crazy how much they look alike though." He shakes his head. "Sorry to bother you. Have a good night." He tilts his bottle in my direction then heads for the far end of the bar where he joins another guy.

"Barb! Come dance!" Cami is bouncing from foot-to-foot like she's in one of those step classes. That girl has far too much energy. Makes me tired just watching her. "Come on!" Mum and Jen have joined them, and it's just me standing on the outside. I guess this is the "fun" Sam said I had to have.

CHAPTER THIRTEEN

MATIU

"I can't believe you're hooking up with her." I shoot Cassian a wary look, resisting the urge to shudder.

"Fuck, man. I didn't know. Honestly." Cass thrusts his hand through his hair. "She never said anything."

I snort. "That's no surprise. Probably wanted to catch me off guard." *And it fucking worked.* Of all the times she could pick to come sauntering back into my life, she chooses my goddamn stag do, when my father-in-law to be is there, no less.

"You… want me to end it with her?" *Of course I fucking do.* But one look at the way he's wincing, tells me he doesn't want to do it. Who the fuck am I to stand in his way?

"Look, mate, I'm not about to tell you what to do." I huff out a breath, reaching for another shot. "Just, be careful, okay?"

The relief on his face… I can't even begin to understand it.

That's a lie. I can understand it all too fucking well. Jodi is one of those girls who makes you feel like you're invincible, like you're the only fucking guy in the world for her. She's what Ma would call a charmer. Someone who knows how to get what she wants, and she's bloody good at it too. That's the problem. Poor Cass is under her spell, and he's going to get hurt, I know it. But what can I do? Forbid the guy from seeing her? Everyone knows that's tempting fate. Forbidden fruit always seems sweeter.

"You sure?" He swipes a hand across his jaw, as if he's seriously considering giving her up if I say the word.

"Go nuts, man. Just don't say I didn't warn ya when it comes back to bite you in the arse." I slug back the shot, feeling the burn as it slides down my throat.

Cassian slumps in his seat. "Thanks, Matiu. I really like her." He slaps a hand on the table. "Let me get you a drink."

"About bloody time," Zeb remarks, tossing the bar towel his way. "It's my night off, remember? Chase tail on your own time." He grins, waggling his brows at Cass, whose cheeks flame. The guy has it bad. "I'll have a bourbon with a vodka shot to chase it down." He clicks his fingers, and Cassian gives him the one finger salute before sliding in behind the bar.

"That was… mature of you." Holden elbows me. "Barb really has changed you." I give him a look, and he holds a hand up placatingly. "In a good way, I mean. The Matiu I knew back in the day would've had old lover boy there by the scruff of the neck."

"And then he'd have me to contend with," Stubbs interjects, pointing a finger in my direction, as if I actually had bailed him up. "We're a family, right? I don't care how good the pussy is, you don't let it come between you."

I glance towards Marty, who's sitting quietly, and I wonder what he's thinking of all this.

Holden snorts mid-sip, then coughs, leaning forward as beer drips from his nose. "You can't say shit like that when I have my mouth full, man." He swipes a hand across his face, mopping up what's left.

Marty pulls a tissue from his pocket and hands it to Holden. He's too pure for this place, too wholesome.

Stubbs raises a questioning brow. "What? You don't think an old-timer like me understands the bro code?" He shakes his head. "Jesus H Christ, I was chasing pussy before you were even born." He nudges Marty with his elbow, as if they go way back. "Right?"

Marty's eyes raise. I doubt he's ever even used the word pussy in his life, but he nods all the same.

Holden chuckles. "I don't doubt it for a second. Just didn't expect to hear those words coming from your mouth. You're normally so…" He glances at me for help, but I'm having far too much fun watching him talk his way out.

"So?" Stubbs prompts with a smirk.

"I don't know. Respectful?"

"Damn right I am. But that doesn't mean I wasn't young once. Doesn't mean I wasn't a horndog chasing tail like you lot before you settled down." He shrugs. "My point is, Jodi isn't worth a bust up between you boys. Girls like her, who fuck around on people, they don't deserve the same respect I give every other woman out there." He glances in my direction. "No offence."

"Shiiiit, man. None taken. You don't have to tell me. She damn near ruined me." *Why the fuck did I just admit that in front of Marty?* I tip back another shot, letting the alcohol do its work and numb everything.

"Until Barb came along and knocked you for a six, right, mate?" Zeb slaps a hand on my shoulder, chuckling. "When she jumped in and kissed you, Jodes was livid. *Livid.*"

"Jesus, Zeb. I didn't even know you knew words like that." Holden jostles him with his elbow. Zeb lunges towards him, but Holden's too quick. He wraps his arm around Zeb's neck and has him in a headlock, rubbing his fist against his head until he taps out.

He bounces up, backing away and adjusting his vest. "One of these days, man, you won't be so quick." He points a finger at Holden, but his lips curl into a grin as he does a little shuffle dance like he's Mohamed Ali.

Zeb may be all talk most of the time, but he's not wrong. Barb *did* throw my world off kilter with that kiss, and the fact it was what finally cemented into Jodi that I wasn't interested anymore was an added bonus. That girl was like a fucking leech, sucking me dry and never letting go. I thought I was rid of her for good, but with Cassanova pining over her, it's pretty clear fate has other plans.

Fuck it. I'm not about to let her sweep back in and take hold again. Cass can have her so long as he keeps her the fuck away from me. Tonight is meant to be about me and the boys, not a bunch of ladies talking about their feelings. I signal Cass with a wave of my hand. "Shots. Now." It's time to put the past where it belongs and move on.

Chapter Fourteen

Barb

"What the actual fuck?" a woman's voice bellows from across the room. Her eyes are narrowed into slits as she stares in my direction, her arms folded across her chest.

"You know her?" Sam asks, coming to stand beside me.

"Nope. Not a fucking clue."

"She looks like she wants to bite your head off." Sam's head bobs as she looks her up and down. "Pretty sure she could too."

The woman has raven black hair and a weathered face. Her shoulders are broad, and her thighs look as though they could snap a man in half. She points at me, then turns her hand, crooking her finger.

What the actual fuck, alright. Jutting my chin up, I make my way over to her. If this bitch wants to fight, she picked the wrong person.

"Stop right there, slut." She holds her hand up, and I stop before her words register.

I run my tongue along my teeth, sucking in a breath before letting it out slowly. "Look, lady, I don't know who the fuck you think I am, but I assure you, I'm not her."

Her eyes widen, along with her stance. "You're gonna look me in the eyes and tell me you're not sleeping with him?"

I throw my hands in the air. "Who?"

She flicks her gaze to my chest and back again. "Who the fuck do you think?"

Not this again.

"Yeah, I *am* sleeping with him. How is it any of your business?" I fold my arms across my chest, my hip cocked.

"Are you kidding me right now? That—" She pokes a finger into my chest, and I take a step back before squaring up to her. "—is my—"

"Woah, woah, woah!" The Māori guy from earlier comes jogging over. "Shazza, I know what it looks like, but you're wrong."

She turns on him. "You're his best mate, Darren, of course you're gonna say that. How stupid do you think I am?"

"Look closer, Shaz. Anaru is a good-looking bloke, but he hasn't had a baby face like that in thirty years. And look at the eyes."

She stares at him for a beat before leaning in so close I can feel her hot breath through my tee. "Ever heard of Photoshop, dumbarse? You can make anyone look good with that."

Fuck this. I take a step back, pointing at my chest. "This is my *fiancé.* Matiu. And apparently the doppelganger to your Anaru." I roll my eyes. "Now can everyone please stop staring at my tits?"

As if on cue, a burly guy with green eyes and a crop of dark hair walks through the door. He has a ta moko from below his nose down to his chin. It's like looking into one of those fun house mirrors, only instead of showing a short, squat version, it's like I'm looking into the future. *Matiu's* future. The resemblance is uncanny.

Shazza spins to face him, her shoulders heaving. Anaru recoils, a look of confusion on his face, and I can't help feeling sorry for him. He has no idea what he's walked into.

"Care to explain?" She folds her arms across her chest, and Anaru holds his hands up, placatingly.

"Sure. What exactly am I explaining?" His eyes dart to his mate then me then Shazza. "What did I miss?"

"Ah, it would seem there's been a misunderstanding," Jen speaks up from behind me. "We're from out of town, here for a hen's do." She wraps her arm around my shoulder, protectively. "Our Barb is getting hitched, aren't you, chicky?" She gives me a squeeze, her smile as bright as ever.

I nod, unable to form words as my eyes find their way back to Anaru.

"Riiiight," he draws the word out, reaching a hand up to scratch the back of his neck. "I still don't fol—" His gaze locks onto my chest, his brow furrowed. "Ah…" He glances up at me. "Is that—?" He huffs out a breath, shaking his head. "Somebody please explain what the hell is going on here."

Finally managing to find my voice, I repeat what I've been saying all night. "I am engaged to Matiu." I point at the big goofball's face. "Who, I can now understand, looks a hell of a lot like you." I squint my eyes. "But your tatt is different." I gesture to his face. "The shade is lighter, and the curves don't match." I tug at my top for the umpteenth time. "See?"

This time Shazza seems to really take notice, her intense gaze scrutinising the image before she nods. "Okay, yeah, I see it." Her lips pull down at the sides and she takes a step back. "Shit, I'm sorry." She cocks her head towards Anaru. "He had a reputation back in the day. I thought… Shit, you know what I thought. How about I buy you all a drink to make up for ruining your night?"

Mum snorts. "It'll take more than *one* drink for that."

I bite the inside of my cheek to stop the eyeroll. "Ignore her. A drink would be great."

"What's your poison?"

"Vodka!" Mum pipes up again, and I quickly shake my head.

"Whiskey."

98

"A gal after my own heart." Shazza offers a smile. "Coming right up."

She makes her way over to the bar, and as she passes, I notice Anaru staring at me intently. I narrow my eyes, cocking my hip.

"Where did you say you're from?" he asks, rubbing at the scruff on his jaw.

"I didn't."

"Brookhaven," Cami blurts out. "We're from Brookhaven."

He swallows, and it looks as though there's something lodged in his throat for all the effort it takes him. He shakes his head, muttering under his breath before his mate grabs him by the arm and drags him over to the bar where the rest of them wait.

"Well, that was weird." Cami stares after Anaru, her lips pursed. "Right?"

"This whole night has been weird," I say, tamping down the unease in the pit of my stomach.

"I'll say, chicky." There's a strange timbre to Jen's voice, and when I look at her, she's twirling a lock of hair around her finger absentmindedly, her eyes set firmly on Darren.

I quirk a brow. "Well, well, well." I can't hide the smirk forming on my lips as I bump her with my hip. "Is that hearts I see in your eyes, Jen?"

"What?" She straightens, her cheeks colouring. "Don't be silly." But her flirty eyes betray her as they find their way back to him.

"Aww, Jen." Sam beams, taking hold of her elbow. "Go over and say hi. He seems like a nice guy."

99

"I mean, he did spend an awful long time staring at my tits earlier, but whatever floats your boat." I snort.

"Shhh," Sam hushes me, a devilish grin on her face. "We're here to have some fun, aren't we? What happens in Hanmer, stays in Hanmer." She gives Jen a little shove.

"I don't know…"

"Oh for Christ's sake." Mum huffs out a breath and grabs hold of Jen, dragging her across the room. I stifle a laugh as Jen looks back at me in terror. For once, I'm on Mum's side. It's been far too long since Jen has let loose.

I shrug, holding my palms up like, *what can you do?*

Mum taps Darren on the shoulder, and when he turns around, he's all smiles and charm. Jen giggles, her fingers toying with her hair again. Anyone would think she was sixteen instead of three times that. I guess it's kind of sweet. In all the years I've been working for her, I don't think I've ever seen her react this way to a man before.

I watch as Mum says something to make Darren's eyes widen, before slapping Jen on the butt and turning on her heel to march back to us. Whatever she said has done the trick though. Darren has his hand on the small of Jen's back, leading her to the bar. At least some good has come out of this night.

Hellhounds MC

Chapter Fifteen

Matiu

"Get your sorry arse outta bed. We've got shit to do." Fists rap along the bench, and I hurl a cushion in that direction. Holden chuckles, and I hear the jug boiling and him moving around the kitchen. How is he whistling like his head isn't about to explode? My head is pounding from that last round of shots. Hell, who am I kidding? It wasn't just the last round that did it. I lost count after ten.

Rolling to my side, I swing my legs off the couch and wince. It seems my head isn't the only thing in pain this morning. "Fuck," I hiss, inspecting the gash along my calf. A vague memory of Zeb coaxing me to ride the creeper like a skateboard flits through my mind. Arsehole.

Dried blood is caked down one side of my leg, and the couch has suffered from a similar fate.

"Don't worry. Zeb came out much worse off than you." Holden holds a steaming cup of coffee out to me, and I take it gratefully. There's nothing like a shot of caffeine to ease a throbbing head.

"Yeah?" I ask, my interest piqued. Serves him right for goading me.

"Yeah. Banged his hip and elbow up good, and Aldrin's gonna have a thing or two to say to him when he comes in." He waggles his brows in amusement.

"Oh shit. Not the Bel-Air."

Holden nods slowly. "Yup." He pops the p. "Took out the left brake light. This far away," he holds his thumb and forefinger up, "to scratching the paintwork. I honestly don't know how it didn't. Lucky son of a bitch."

Lucky alright. That car will be driving Barb to the wedding in two weeks, and if anything happened to take that away, there'd be hell to pay. Especially now I know why it's so important to her.

"He can be the one to break it to Aldrin when he comes in to pick it up Monday morning." I snicker. Aldrin is as gentle as a lamb until you fuck with his four-wheeled babies. I learned that one the hard way. I'd only been at Lawson's Lugs a few weeks when he brought in an Impala, wanting it tuned and detailed. Jeri tossed me the keys and told me to take extra care, and me being the numbnuts that I was at eighteen, I didn't listen. Took it out for a joyride one night after work—the temptation had been too much—and I had a little run in with the gutter, taking a corner too sharp. Scratched up the hubcaps on the passenger side and the thought never occurred to me to buff them out before he came to collect. Jericho hit me up first thing in the morning and said I'd have to talk to Aldrin and tell him what I did. The bastard knew what he was setting me up for and gave me no fucking warning either. Just sent me to the wolf like a lamb to slaughter. I thought I knew what rage was, but shit was I wrong. Aldrin hit the fucking roof. Had me up against the wall, his face all red and nostrils flaring. I damn near shit my pants. It was what I pictured it would be like to get in trouble with your old man. Jeri stepped in and talked him down, gave him a discount or something, and he's never raised so much as a finger at me again. Of course, I've never crossed the line and taken a car out when I shouldn't again either. And I make sure to take extra good care when it's one of Aldrin's cars in the lot. That's for damn sure.

"That's cold." Holden chuckles. He hasn't experienced one of Aldrin's rages, but he's heard about them enough to know.

"Serves the fucker right. I could've broken my ankle doing that shit. Then he'd have Barb to contend with too." I love her, but she's one feisty chick. You get on her bad side and you know about it. Hell, I almost lost her because I was a dumb shit. Throwing my weight around like she couldn't be without me, when in reality, it was the other way around. Thank Christ she gave me another chance. It wasn't until I could've lost her for good that it really sunk in.

Fuck, when I think about the danger I put her in when we went after Dante, it sets my soul alight. Not that I could've stopped her. She was going whether I wanted her to or not. But still, the thought of anything happening to her, especially on my watch, is too much. It does fucked up things to my heart. Makes it go off kilter or something. Like it would stop beating if she weren't here, by my side. It's fucked up that it took that for me to realise, but whatever. She's my ride or die, it's as simple as that. I'd kill for her, and she'd do the same for me. In fact, I'd hate to be Jodi when Barb finds out she was here last night. Like I said, I wouldn't want to fuck with her, and Jodi pushes *all* the wrong buttons.

"Well, it's a good thing you have the balance and grace of a cat, right, bro?" Holden slaps me on the back, and I damn near choke on my mouthful of coffee. "Now get your arse up and dressed. Jeri wants us to go pay Juanita a visit."

"The fuck for? I told Stubbs there's no way she's in on this shit." I set my cup down, my stomach roiling.

Holden holds his hands up. "You don't have to tell me, man. I don't believe it either, but Jeri wants to make sure."

"Meanwhile, Curtis and Murphy are out there doing real damage. They run girls, man. No way Juanita would get into bed with them. No fucking way." Other than Ma, she's the closest thing to a saint that I know. Sure, she had it rough growing up, but that's exactly why I know she wouldn't be in on this. You don't get forced into prostitution when you're thirteen to then turn around and okay the same thing happening to other girls. You just don't.

"Which is why we need to get this out of the way. We prove she has nothing to do with this, and we can move onto other ways of getting this scum out of Brookhaven."

He makes a good point. I get that Jeri wants to clean house and has to check all bases, but on this, he's wrong, and if I have to hit up Juanita to prove it, I will.

"Yeah, alright. Gimme five to shower first."

Holden raises his brows, the corners of his mouth turned up into a smirk. "Make it ten, bro. You smell like a brewery dipped in stale smoke." He wafts his hand in front of his nose to get his point across. Smart prick.

"Like you're a garden of roses." I shake my head, but he's not wrong; I *do* smell like I've been soaking in whiskey all night.

We pull up outside Juanita's place. It hasn't changed much over the years aside from a little paint chipping on the white picket fence out front. The lawn is neatly manicured with some of those small hedges lining the path up to the front door. It's definitely not the home of a woman behind a human trafficking agency. Though, I suppose, if she was, it would be the perfect way to hide it. Goddamn it. Jeri's getting inside my head.

I knock on the door then take a step back, waiting. Holden stands on the step behind me, his hands clasped in front of him.

Footsteps pad towards the door before it swings open, and Juanita beams at me. "Matiu, what a nice surprise." Her smile falters when she notices I'm not alone, and a slight frown forms. "Is everything okay?"

I clear my throat, raising my hand to rub at the back of my neck. This is awkward as shit. "Ah, yeah, we just need to talk to you, clear up a little misunderstanding, is all."

"Okay?" She steps aside. "Would you like to come in?"

Chapter Sixteen

Barb

The front door rattles followed by a hiss of profanities. I set my coffee down and pad towards the door, pulling it open with a flourish. "Forget your key, Jen?"

Her cheeks flush and she brushes a hand through her hair before pushing past me and into the lounge, where she's greeted with applause.

"Oh shut up," she says, slapping her hands to her face and shaking her head.

Sam comes up behind, wrapping her arms around Jen's middle and resting her chin on her shoulder. "Don't be embarrassed. We think it's great."

"About fucking time, is what it is," I say with a smirk.

Jen gives me a look like she's trying to scold me, but the glint in her eye betrays her. She's happy, glowing even.

"Okay, spill." Cami folds her legs beneath her, patting the couch cushion beside her. "We want alllllll the details, right, ladies?" She waggles her brows, and it's like we all turn into teenagers, gathering around Jen with grins on our faces. Even my mother gets in on it. "Don't leave anything out."

"A lady doesn't kiss and tell," she says coyly, and I snort.

"Good thing you're not a lady then, eh?" She swats at me.

"Actually, it's gentlemen who never kiss and tell," Darcy adds. "Ladies can do whatever they want."

"She's got you there." Mum crosses one leg over the other, her hands clasped over her knee. "And I, for one, expect a blow-by-blow account of your evening. I mean, I *did* push you two together after all." She brushes lint off her knee, twisting her lips to the side. "Now give us the tea."

"Geez, chickies. Anyone would think you haven't got anything better to discuss than a middle-aged woman's sex life."

"Yussss!" Cami bounces in her seat, clapping her hands. "Get it, girl!"

"I think I might have, chicky." Jen's grin is wide, her eyes lit up like a kid at Christmas. "If 'get it' means what I think it does."

"Jesus, Jen, you're not that old. Of course it does." I roll my eyes, but secretly, I'm happy for her.

Cami holds her hand up for a high-five, and Jen obliges with a chuckle. "Sooo, are you gonna see him again?"

"I might." Jen fluffs her hair. "But we live in different towns, so…"

"So what? You don't have to live in each other's pockets, Jen. Honestly." My mother lifts her coffee to her lips with a smirk. "Take it from me, there's a lot of fun to be had with no strings."

"I think I just threw up in my mouth." I swallow back the vile taste with a shake of my head. The last thing I want to hear about is my mother's sex life. "Gross."

"Pfft, it wasn't gross when you were asking her what she got up to." She points at Jen.

"Yeah, well, that's different. She didn't give birth to me."

"And how do you think that came about in the first place? Immaculate conception?" She raises her brows at me, like she's actually expecting me to answer that.

"There's a difference between knowing something happened and hearing about it firsthand. No one needs to know what shady shit their mum gets up to in her own time."

"I may be your mother, but I'm still a woman with needs."

"Ugh, stop." This time I can't stop the gag reflex and fling a hand across my mouth. My eyes water, and I have to swallow a few times to make sure everything stays where it belongs. Why is she like this?

109

Darcy's eyes keep flitting between me and Mum, her teeth chewing on her lower lip as if she's not sure what to do or how to take us, and I have to remind myself to be civil. It's one more night. I can do this.

"Anyway," I say drily, securing Jen with an imploring stare. "Come on, give us the dirt." I roll my hand in the air.

Jen perches on the edge of the couch, her hands clasped and pushed between her thighs. Closing her eyes, she grins. "It was…"

"Huge?" Cami cuts in, chuckling.

Jen's cheeks flush, and everyone takes that as a yes and cheers. She fans her hands in front of her face. "Oh my gosh, you guys!" She giggles. Actually giggles like she's sixteen, then she nods, hiding her face in her hands. "It was though."

"Okay, but are we talking length or girth? Because that makes a difference." Cami holds her pointer fingers out with a ruler length between them. She waggles her brows, and Jen's eyes widen.

"Good God, chicky, how big do you think Mary-Jane is?"

"Ahh, I feel I'm going to regret this, but… who the hell is Mary-Jane?" I wince, anticipating the answer.

She snorts, giving me a look like I'm delusional, then points to her crotch. "Mary-Jane." She glances around the room, then laughs, folding her arms across her chest. "You haven't named yours?"

"No, can't say I have."

Darcy and Sam both shake their head no, but Cami pipes up with, "Monaro, cos she's expensive to fill, but she'll purr if you treat her right."

I snort out a laugh, and Cami grins. "It's true though!"

"Patsy," Mum says. "Because she's absolutely fabulous."

This time Jen cracks up laughing, while the rest of us have no idea what they're on about. I'm more disturbed by the fact she has a name for it. She's always seemed so up herself, for want of a better phrase, and definitely not the type to name her vajeen. It's like I don't even know who she is anymore.

"You still haven't answered the question," Cami sings, wiggling her fingers in the air.

Jen pushes them closer together. "Mary-Jane doesn't need an anaconda, chicken. And if they know what they're doing, Monaro shouldn't either. It's all in the way they use it." Jen winks.

"So it was good then?" she prompts. Anyone would think she had money riding on it, she's that invested.

"He was gentle and made sure to see to my needs before his own, and afterwards, he held me and we fell asleep like that. Me tucked up under his arm." She smiles wistfully.

"Aww." Darcy holds her hand to her chest. "That's so sweet."

Sounds like a snoozefest to me. Give me hot and heavy any day of the week. None of this making love bullshit. I want it raw and hard. I want to feel like I've

111

been fucked and not handled like I'm some sort of dainty flower. I don't want to be cherished. I want to be claimed.

"I'm so happy for you," Sam gushes. "I don't think I've seen you smile like that before."

Jen ducks her head like the demure lady she's not. "It's been a long time since I've felt cared for like that. It was nice."

"Well that's decidedly mushy. I think we need to liven things up a bit before I start going soft." I shudder.

"We could walk up the hill," Darcy suggests, and I give her the dirtiest look I can. Her shoulders slump inwards, and I instantly feel bad. "Or not."

"We haven't had a lot of time to get to know each other, but me and exercise, unless it's of the—" I glance sidewards at my mother, "—kinky kind, we don't get on all that well."

Her cheeks flame, but she nods in understanding.

"The hot pools?" Sam quirks a brow. "We got you a voucher for a massage, and we could all get manicures while we're there."

Not exactly the lively activity I had in mind, but it does sound like a good way to waste a few hours before the drinking can commence. "Sure, but I draw the line at pedicures though. Ain't nobody touching my feet."

HELLHOUNDS MC

CHAPTER SEVENTEEN

MATIU

"Please tell me you're joking?" I pace the length of Juanita's living room floor and back again. "I defended you. I told them there was no way you'd be involved in something like this."

"Look, I knew you wouldn't understand, and that's exactly why I didn't tell you. And, quite frankly, Matiu, it's none of your damn business." She leans back, folding her arms across her chest.

"None of my business? I'm in the Hellhounds! We had an understanding, or so I thought. Are you saying you no longer want the Hellhounds to help you out?"

"That's not what I'm saying, and you know it. Would you sit down, please? You're making me nervous with all that pacing."

Begrudgingly, I take a seat opposite her.

"Maybe you could explain it to us," Holden suggests, even though there's no explanation good enough for the mayor to allow human trafficking in our town.

Juanita sighs, scrubbing a hand over her face. "You know how my teenage years played out. It's not something I would ever wish on anyone. Doped up to the eyeballs, spinning tricks all hours of the day and night to get my next fix. It wasn't a pretty time. It was Celeste who got me out, did you know that?"

I shake my head no. I've heard the stories of that time, but for whatever reason, they never told me it was Ma who'd saved her. Though, come to think of it, it makes sense. The bond they have, they're the closest thing to sisters I've ever seen without blood being involved.

"What you probably don't know is that Sarah went through a pretty rough patch when she was a little younger than you are now. She went off the rails and I couldn't get through to her, no matter what I did."

I'd heard them talk about her daughter a time or two, but it was always kind of hush-hush. She took off before I was born, and as far as I know, she's never come back.

Her lips tremble as she sucks in a breath. "She was following down the same path as me, spinning tricks to pay for her addiction. Only she didn't have someone like Celeste to help her. I wouldn't fund her habit, so she shut me out. I couldn't reach her." Tears fill her eyes, and I have to look away. I can't stay mad at her when she's looking so vulnerable like this.

"Jesus." Holden sits back in his seat. "That's rough."

"You have no idea. The terror you feel as a mother watching your child fall apart before your eyes and there's nothing you can do." She shakes her head. "It's unbearable. I damn near fell off the wagon myself."

I know that can't have been easy for her to admit. She's always prided herself in her rise out of the ashes. Bad girl turned good.

"I spent years trying to get her clean. Put her in rehab, but she'd last a day or two before running away. I can't tell you how many times the Hellhounds would be out scouting around for her. Both Tony and Stubbs marched her right back home with her tail between her legs a time or two. And a few where she fought them tooth and nail too." She shakes her head, dropping it into her hands.

"When I found her on the bathroom floor, foaming at the mouth and unresponsive, I thought I'd lost her. They pumped her stomach and kept watch over her for days while she went through withdrawals. One of the hardest times of my life. The agonising pain I knew she was going through, and I had to just stand by and watch."

Tears spill down her cheeks, and she brushes them away. "It took a while, but we got her through it.

115

She even started seeing someone for a short time, and I thought I had her back. My baby." She frowns, closes her eyes and takes a deep breath. I know what's coming next. This part I remember.

"I put too much pressure on her to stay well. Fussed over her too much. Kept a close eye on her, and in the end, she couldn't handle it anymore. She vanished in the middle of the night. Left me a note saying she couldn't handle seeing the suspicion in my eyes." She shakes her head, staring out the window. "I pushed her away."

"Nita—"

She holds her hand up to stop me. "Don't. I know what I did, and I have to live with that. I don't want anyone else to have to go through that. To have to bear the pain of their child running away and never knowing if they're okay, if they're safe." Her voice drops to a whisper. "If they're even alive."

The room falls silent but for her sniffles. I look over to Holden, who gives me a wide-eyed stare.

"I understand where you're coming from."

She scoffs. "You have no idea."

"You're right, I don't. Sorry, that was a dumb thing to say."

Holden snorts, and I shoot him a look. I don't see him jumping in to say anything.

"I just mean, it makes sense what you're saying. Having a safe place for these girls, rather than leaving them to fend for themselves against the dickheads of the world, it makes sense." I lean forward, forcing her to meet my gaze. "But how much do you know about these guys, Nita? Because I don't think they're who you think they are."

"I haven't looked into them. They approached council with a business plan and asked for consent. I invited them here to give a presentation and talk it through. They seem legit."

"They are far from it, ma'am," Holden interjects. "We had a run in with them just last year."

Her eyes narrow. "What kind of run in?"

"They were trying to run drugs through Brookhaven. They didn't get very far though. We saw to that."

Her head whips around so fast, and she hits me with that look that mums get. That one that makes you feel the size of an ant. "Why am I only hearing of this now?"

"Like he said, we took care of it. I didn't think it was necessary until now." I suck in a breath, knowing this next part will be the kicker. "There's more. We've uncovered a trafficking ring they had going a while back. Somehow they managed to keep their names out of it and didn't see any time for it, but they were involved. One hundred percent."

Juanita's face pales. "Oh Jesus, what have I done? I gave them the go-ahead. Passed it on to council with my recommendation."

"Can't you like, call it back or something? Say you changed your mind?"

"I don't..." She pushes to her feet, shaking her hands out in front of her. "I gave my approval. I can't go back on that. Not without cause."

"Okay, let me talk to Jeri. Maybe he has some ideas. We'll find a way out of this, Nita. I promise."

Chapter Eighteen

Barb

"You have a lot of tension in your lower back. We tend to carry our unexpressed anger here, which makes it tight and uncomfortable." The masseuse indicates a spot on her spine, the same spot she spent a good deal of time kneading in my back moments ago. "You could try some stretches to help relieve that, and breathing exercises to help let go of some of that pent-up anger. Have you got a lot going on at the moment?" she asks with a sympathetic smile.

I huff out a laugh. "Lady, you have no idea." I take a gulp of the cool water she handed me before continuing. "I'm getting married in a few weeks. This is my hen's weekend." I wave my hand around the room.

"Oh, how lovely. Congratulations."

"Thanks."

"It's understandable you'd be stressed out. Can your partner give you a hand with anything? Help take the pressure off?"

"Oh, the wedding isn't what's stressing me out." I shake my head. "My mother is. She can be… difficult to deal with." She nods, and I continue, the damn breaking. "We don't really see eye-to-eye. She left my dad in some sort of mid-life crisis, and now she spends her days drinking and sleeping her way around whatever town she's in at the time." I roll my eyes, taking another gulp of water, then wiping my mouth with my sleeve. "And she takes any opportunity to point out how much she despises the idea of me marrying Matiu." I tip the water back again, finishing the glass before slamming it on the desk.

The masseuse blinks at me, clearing her throat.

Clawing my hands through my hair, I mumble an apology. I guess I did have a lot of pent-up anger.

"It's okay. It's natural for these feelings to come out after a massage." She leans in. "I have a mother-in-law who sounds very similar, so I get it."

For her sake, I hope not. The idea of there being another of my mother out there is frightening. One is plenty, and even that is too much sometimes.

I toss her the voucher and a nod of thanks before padding out the door and towards the pools. The air is cool outside, enough to tease my breath into visible tendrils. Scanning the pools, I spot Jen and Mum in one of the smaller pools, leaned up against the boulders lining the edge. Two young men lounge between them, my mother's arm draped casually around the shoulders of one. I fight back the urge to turn on my heels and leave them all behind and make my way over.

"Darling!" Mum calls, waving her fingers in the air. "Come meet our friends."

Jen gives me an apologetic smile, and I know exactly what's going on before my mother even opens her mouth.

"This here is Jonty." She pats the golden-skinned one on the chest, giving him a half-lidded stare before turning to his companion. "And this is Marcus." She takes his chin between her thumb and finger. "He just moved to a place right outside of Brookhaven, didn't you, Marcus?"

His eyes rake the length of my body before settling on my tits. "Yes, ma'am." He licks his lips, and once again I find myself suppressing a shudder. Whatever she's told him, he's sadly mistaken.

"Maybe you two could get together and you could show him around?" Her eyes glint as she flashes me the smile that seems to make men drop to their knees for her. Honestly, I don't see the appeal.

"Thanks, but no thanks. I'm a little busy with the *wedding*." I make sure to say it loud and clear, holding up my ring finger and meeting Marcus's gaze to drive the point home. Taken, and not interested.

Mum scowls like I've just taken a shit in her cereal. But whatever. She needs to realise this isn't going away. I'm marrying Matiu whether she likes it or not.

Marcus laughs awkwardly, and the two make their excuses and wade away.

"You could've been a bit more hospitable, you know." She folds her arms sullenly. "Would it hurt you to be nice to people every once in a while?"

I quirk a brow. "Our versions of nice are very different, Mum."

She flaps her hand through the air. "Can you blame a mother for wanting what's best for her daughter?"

I run my tongue along my teeth, sucking in a deep breath like the masseuse suggested. "What makes you think you know what's best for me? You don't think I'm capable of making my own decisions?"

"I don't think that's what she was meaning, right, Sandra?" Jen stands, water sluicing from her body in rivulets. She turns to Mum. "We're here for a good, relaxing time, remember?"

It's like she never uttered a word though. Mum's eyes remain glued to mine, her jaw tight as she clenches her teeth. "I know best because I raised you. I know you better than you know yourself."

"I highly doubt that."

"What exactly are you trying to say here, Barbara? You think I'm a lousy mother, is that it?"

"I'm sure that's not—"

"If the shoe fits."

Her jaw drops, and she stands, pointing a finger at me. "You ungrateful cow! Everything I've done, I've done for you."

122

"Oh really? You left dad and decided to become a slut for my benefit, did you?"

Mum rears back as if I slapped her, and I suppose I did, in a way.

"I don't expect you to understand all the sacrifices I made for you over the years, but there were plenty. Excuse me for wanting to take some of my youth back and have a little fun while I still can."

"A little fun I could handle, but you're making a fool of yourself. Throwing yourself at men half your age, sleeping with anyone who pays you attention. It's embarrassing."

"Guys, come on," Jen pleads. I know we're drawing far too much attention, but I'm in it now and I'm not about to back down. Whatever that masseuse did to me, it released something, and I need to get it all out.

"I'm sorry you find me embarrassing. Right now, I think you're the one embarrassing yourself, and you're only going to go and do it again if you walk down that aisle in a few weeks."

"You know nothing of what I have with Matiu," I say between gritted teeth. "You haven't even bothered to give him a chance and get to know him."

"He's in a gang, for Christ's sake! No mother in their right mind would accept that as an okay match for their daughter. You may not believe it, but I'm trying to stop you from making a huge mistake. I don't want you to regret things like I…" Her voice trails off and she looks away.

"Like you did?" I say bitterly. She made it quite clear when she left Dad that she never would've married him if it wasn't for me coming along when I did. "Wow. Mother of the year." I clap slowly, though inside it feels as though every part of me is shattering into tiny pieces.

She huffs out a sigh. "I don't mean you. I could never regret you."

"You regretting Dad is the same thing. There is no me without him."

She shakes her head. "You always take his side. I'm here, aren't I? I'm with you even though I don't abide by it. What more do you want from me?"

"I want you to give a shit about how *I* feel. You look at Matiu and see a mistake, but I look at him and see my best friend. Someone who challenges me and would go to the end of the Earth to protect me." I swipe at my cheeks, hot with angry tears. "You think I'm judging you for enjoying life, but look who I learned from. You judged Matiu the second you saw him."

Her voice is low when she speaks again, her eyes brimming with tears. I'd feel guilty if I weren't so fucking angry with her. "I only want what's best for you. It's all I've ever wanted."

I fight to keep the derision from my voice. "Then why can't you trust me when I say he's it for me?" She goes to speak, but I hold my hand up, stopping her. "Because he is, Mum. He's who I choose to be with, and he'll still be who I choose to be with twenty years from now. Matiu is it for me, and you either need to accept that or..." I pull myself up to my full height, meeting her with a steely gaze. "Or you don't come to the wedding."

HELLHOUNDS MC

CHAPTER NINETEEN

MATIU

"Absolutely not." Jericho stares me down, his arms folded across his chest. "That's not what the Hellhounds are about."

"Shiiit, Jeri, I know that, and I'm not asking us to get into bed with Curtis and Murphy. What I'm saying is, we push them out, take over the business ourselves." I lean back in my chair, lighting a cigarette and taking a drag. "We could have one of our boys on as security and we find someone we trust to run the desk." I look to Holden. "Maybe Darce? Or Cami?"

He snorts. "You're fucking dreaming if you think I'm getting Darcy involved in anything like that. She's been through enough without having to deal with dick knobs who want to get their end away. No dice, man."

"Okay, yeah." I scrub a hand down my face. "I see your point, but Cami don't take shit from anyone. She'd be perfect."

He tilts his head in consideration.

"This isn't up for discussion. We are not, and never will be, involved in running girls, end of story." Jericho leans forward, steepling his hands on the table in front of him.

"Now, Jeri, as much as I hate to admit it, the boy may be onto something here." Stubbs raises his hand to stop Jeri from interjecting. "Listen, what I think he's meaning by all this, is that we don't run the business the way they want it run, we do it our way. Am I right?"

"Yeah."

"Right, so it's a place where woman who want to, can offer services, and men will pay to enjoy those services. We're there to keep it on the up and up, and we look after the girls. They don't end up on drugs or walking the streets, and we make some money on the side." He twists his hands palms up. "Seems like a win win situation to me."

Jeri stares him down. "So you're on board with this?"

"I think we can make it work, yeah. Look, we want to keep these girls safe, right? And we know this shit is happening here already, but this way we can keep an eye on it, and shitheads like Montgomery won't get a foot in the door."

"Fuck." Jeri shakes his head. "Holden?"

"It does make sense, man. And this way Juanita doesn't get left with egg on her face when it falls to pieces – which it would with those fucktards running it."

"And you know Juanita would help us out. She's got as much to lose and gain as we do. All she wants is a safe place for these girls, and she thought that's what she was getting with Curtis, but we know that's not how it'll play out." I take another drag. "I really think we can do this."

"You ran it past Barb yet?" Jericho asks with a smirk.

"Shiiit, old man, you think I'm stupid? Like hell I was going to say anything without your go-ahead." I shake my head. "I'm not about to get shot before I reach the damn aisle."

Holden snorts. "Mate, to be a fly on the wall when you tell her."

"Fuck off. Barb's cool. She'll understand what I'm trying to do. I'm just not stupid enough to tell her when she's away."

"Sure. That's what it is." Holden cracks a whip in the air then barks out a laugh.

"Laugh it up, dickhead. You're just as pussy whipped as the rest of us."

Jericho stands, signalling the end of our meeting. "If we're going to do this, I want a meeting with Juanita. We need to make sure we do this right. Holden, you reckon Cami would be keen to be on the books?"

"Are you kidding? She gets to be the gatekeeper and choose who can come in and who has to fuck off. It's right up her alley."

Zeb raises his hand. "I'm happy to be one of the heavies."

Holden raises his brows. "My sister is off limits. How many times do I have to say that?"

"First of all, I didn't say anything about Cami, and secondly, she's a big girl, can't she make her own choices?" He grins, sticking his tongue out between his teeth. "And if I'm there 24/7, kicking out the losers, I'll look like a great fucking choice." He darts out of the way of Holden's swinging hand. "Come on, you know I'm a better choice than what's out there." He flings his arm towards the streets. "Wouldn't you love to have me as your bro-in-law?"

Holden snarls, taking another swing at the back of his head and missing. "Don't fucking push it."

"Ah." Cassian coughs, raising his hand. "What about Jodi? Could she, like, have a job there too?"

"No fucking way," I say, stubbing out my cigarette. "Have your fun with her, whatever, but this is business. Trust me, we don't want her involved."

Cass shoots Jericho a look, but he's met with a shake of the head. "Sorry, bro. I agree with Matiu on this one. She's a liability."

"What would she do anyway?" Zeb pipes up. "Strip? Service men? Sure you'd love knowing your old lady is sleeping with half the men of Brookhaven."

"Dick, I meant behind the desk."

"Behind the desk, on the desk, it's all the same to her, right, Matiu?" Zeb's eyes dance with laughter, and Holden looks as though he's about ready to burst too.

I shoot Cass a look of apology. "I mean, they're not wrong."

"Fuck you guys. Jodi is a sweetheart. She hasn't done anything wrong."

"Ah, you forgotten crawling behind the bar with a black eye the other day?" I ask, because someone's got to get through to him.

"That's not the same thing."

"Isn't it?"

"They had broken up, and he didn't like that she'd moved on." He shrugs like it's no big deal that his old lady got him hurt.

"Believe me, when it comes to Jodes, there's most certainly more to it than that. She's a serial cheater. She moves on but keeps you dangling, and then when you find out, she makes it your fault." I tap out another cigarette. "And once you give her the flick, she'll keep her claws in you until you make it so she can't."

Holden sucks in a breath, his eyes flicking between me and Cass, who's staring at me with daggers.

"Look, man, I don't want to start a fight. Maybe she's different now, I don't know, and I don't want to know. But I hope, for you, that she is. All I know is that I wouldn't trust her with a ten-foot fucking pole."

CHAPTER TWENTY

BARB

"Barb, Barb!" Jen runs out the door after me, her jandals flapping loudly. "Come on, Barb, you don't mean that." She grabs hold of my wrist, pulling me to a stop. I shake my hand free, fumbling in my bag for a cigarette.

"Hey, got a light?" I ask a passing teen. He holds up his vape and shrugs. "Of fucking course." I huff and stomp across the road to the Four Square.

Jen is still dripping wet from the hot pool, so she hangs back outside, but I see her pacing back and forth through the door. She's wearing only a bikini and jandals, because she ran straight after me, forgetting about her towel or clothes. She must be freezing. Clearly I've fucked up the whole hens weekend by confronting my mother, but she had it coming. Who suggests their daughter gets together with some rando guys when she's literally getting married in a few weeks' time? An insane person, that's who.

My hand shakes with adrenaline, but somehow I manage to get the lighter to work and suck in a deep breath, letting the nicotine do its thing and calm my nerves. Tilting my head back, I slowly blow smoke into the air, watching it swirl about before evaporating.

"Barb," Jen tries again. "You can't cut your mother out of your wedding."

"The ball is in her court, Jen." I meet her gaze. "All she has to do is stop this bullshit and give him a chance."

"I know, chick, I do. But in her roundabout way, she's only trying to do what she thinks is best for you."

I pinch the bridge of my nose. "Please don't you start in on it too. I thought you liked Matiu?" I hate that my voice is shaking along with my hands. This is not who I am.

"Chicky, come on. You know I love the big lug." She takes my hand, leading me to a bench seat. "But it doesn't matter what I think of him anyway. And it doesn't matter what she thinks of him either. All that matters is how *you* feel." She strokes a hand over my head, a move so motherly it makes me want to cry. Why is it that Jen is out here comforting me instead of my own mother? Why can't she see what she's doing to me?

"You love him, right?" she asks, leaning down to meet my eyes.

"Yeah, I do. I'd go to fucking war for him." I wave my hand towards the pools, as if that's what I've done.

"Then that's all that matters. She'll come around, just give it time. But, chicky, I don't think you want to cut her from your wedding. You'll regret it if you do."

"And what if she pulls another stunt like that? I just ignore it? Laugh it off?" I shake my head. "It fucking hurts that she doesn't trust me to make this decision on my own." I take another shaky drag on my cigarette. "Why can't she try with Matiu like Dad has? She has no idea what kind of man he is."

"No, she doesn't, and that's a shame, but it's her who's missing out, okay? I know this whole business with your folks has really thrown a spanner in the works for you, chicken, and I know you're hurting over it, but she's trying her best."

I snort. "If you say so."

"I'm in no way taking her side here, but she married young, right? Maybe around your age?"

I huff out a sigh, knowing where she's going with this. "Yeah."

"So maybe it's not Matiu himself she's opposed to, but marriage in general. Maybe she's worried you'll change your mind down the track like she did, and she wants to spare you that pain. Whatever her reasons, it's a Sandra problem, okay? It doesn't actually have anything to do with your ability to make a decision or how she feels about Matiu, it's her own worries that she's reflecting back on you."

I toss my cigarette to the ground and stamp it out with my foot. "Jesus, Jen, you watch far too much Dr. Phil."

She laughs. "Probably. Sounded like I knew what I was talking about though, right?" She nudges me with her elbow before swinging an arm around my shoulder.

I lean into her, letting her words soak in.

A small cough sounds from behind us, and I turn to see the rest of our gaggle wrapped in towels and holding out Jen's bag.

"You, um, forgot this," Darcy says, whipping a towel out from the bag and draping it around Jen's shoulders.

"Thanks ladies. I was getting a bit nipply out here." Jen laughs, rubbing her hand up and down my arm before standing and taking her bag from Darcy.

Sam eyes me, one brow raised in question, and I nod to let her know I'm over my little hissy fit. Mum is at the back of the group, her head down as she toys with the zip on her bag.

"Sooo," Cami pipes up, rocking back on her heels. "Anyone up for a drink?"

We find ourselves back at the same pub as the night before. Piled into a booth, our bags all tucked beneath the table, we order a few bowls of fries and a round of cocktails. Mum is on the opposite side of the table, and she still hasn't looked at me. Jen and Cami are doing a great job at pretending everything is sweet as, keeping the chatter going.

"You okay?" Sam leans in and asks on the quiet.

"Yeah. Believe it or not, Jen had some words of wisdom for me, and they actually made sense." I snort out a laugh. It's not that I don't think she's smart; the women has run her own salon for years, so she's obviously savvy when it comes to business; it's that the whole time I've known her, she's never been in a serious relationship, so I guess I didn't expect it. More to the point, I didn't expect it to make so much sense.

I know Mum getting pregnant with me so young wasn't in her plan, and obviously marrying Dad wasn't either, so I guess I can see why she'd be worried about it. All the same, I'm a grown-arse woman who knows her own mind and heart, and even though he can be a right pain in my arse, I wouldn't have anyone else. Matiu is it for me.

"Oooh, if it isn't lover boy," Cami singsongs, pointing a finger towards the door and a red-faced Darren.

"Ah, hi, ladies." He gives us a sheepish wave.

"Come join us." Cami gets up, leaving a space beside Jen. She ushers us across until Sam is practically on my lap so she can squeeze in next to Darce.

"I wouldn't want to intrude on your night." He looks to Jen with hearts in his eyes, and her cheeks flame.

"You're not intruding," she says, patting the seat beside her.

"Well, you don't have to tell me twice." He slides onto the seat, his arm propped up along the back behind Jen, his thumb tracing lines across her shoulder.

I make a point of looking around the room. "Nigel no mates today, are ya, Daz?" I snag a chip and swirl it in the bowl of sauce before popping it into my mouth.

"Ha!" He shuffles in his seat, his arm wrapping firm around Jen. "Afraid so. Anaru had some business out of town to attend to, and the rest are all soft cocks."

"Nobody wants one of those." Cami winks at Jen. "Right?"

"Aaah?" He glances sidewards, and Jen's eyes almost bulge out of her head.

"She doesn't mean you! I never said... I wouldn't... You have nothing to worry about." She goes to pat his leg, but is so flustered her hand lands elsewhere, and his eyes widen. "Oh my god!" Jen buries her face in her hands.

Darren chuckles, pulling her into his side. "You can put your hands on me anytime you like."

Jen curls herself into his chest, peeking up at him. "Really?"

I clear my throat. "I don't know about you, but I could use another drink." I tip mine back, and the others follow suit. "Last big night before the big day, so let's make it count, right?"

Cami gives a whoop as she stands, making room for everyone to pile out and make their way to the bar. Mum sits in the corner, chewing her lip.

"You coming?" I ask, holding my hand out to her.

CHAPTER TWENTY-ONE

MATIU

How long does it take to drive back from Hanmer? Barb messaged to say she was on her way two hours ago, and I'm itching to wrap my arms around her. Goddamn this weekend has been a lot. Having to watch Cass suck face with my ex is not exactly how I thought I'd be spending my Saturday night, but it is what it is. At least I wasn't the only one uncomfortable with it. Even Marty looked like he wanted to be somewhere else, and he doesn't know either of them. It's not that I was jealous or anything, far from it, in fact. It's that I know she's going to hurt him. She's all for show, and for some fucked up reason, she's trying to prove something to me. Like I give a fuck what she does in her spare time. The minute she let someone else touch what I thought was mine, I stopped caring. I'm not into playing games, but that's all Jodi seems to be capable of doing, and I don't know how to make Cass see sense without sounding like a jealous bitch.

Fuck, Barb is going to be pissed when she finds out. I don't want to tell her, but I have to. It's not like Cass is about to hide it from her anyway. He's thinking with a whole other brain right now.

On top of that, I have to run this brothel idea past her too, and I don't know how she's going to take it. It's not every day you ask your Mrs if you can start up a sex joint. Jesus H. Christ, I must have a death wish.

I hear her before I see her, the low rumble of the Holden Commodore we use at Lawson Lugs from time-to-time coasts slowly around the corner, turning into our drive.

Flicking my cigarette across the lawn, I stand up off the steps and march over to her, pulling the door open before she has a chance.

"Well, hello to you too," she says with a grin. She slides her long legs out of the car, her leggings so tight they look painted on.

I take her hands and yank her into my arms, lifting her from the ground. With my head in her neck, I inhale, and instantly I'm at ease.

"Guess you missed me, huh?" She hooks her hand around the nape of my neck, pulling me in for a kiss. "I missed you too," she purrs.

"Fuck." I draw the word out, my forehead pressed to hers. "You have no idea." With one swift motion, I cup my hands beneath her arse and lift her into my arms. Her legs wrap around my waist, and I kick the car door closed as I carry her inside. The bags can wait. I need her. Now.

Pushing her back against the wall, I crush my lips to hers. She sighs into me, her fingers sliding into my hair. She tastes of coffee and something sweet. I bite her lip, and she hisses, closing her eyes and throwing her head back against the wall, giving me access to her neck. My tongue laps at the soft flesh there, landing on her pulse where I press my lips. A whimper falls from her mouth, and she grinds herself against me.

"Not yet, baby." Lifting the hem of her shirt, I slip a hand beneath to find her braless, and I let out a groan as I find her breast. "Fuck."

"Told you I missed you," she pants, leaning in to my ear. "I'm not wearing any panties either."

Sweet Jesus, the things this woman does to me. I run my hand back down to cup her arse, slipping a hand beneath her leggings to feel her smooth, bare skin. She grinds into me again, and it's all I can do not to rip her pants off and fuck her right here, right now.

I slide my hand between her thighs, finding her wet and ready. As I slip one finger inside, she lets out a moan, circling her hips. I add another, stroking the rough spot inside that always makes her gasp.

"Oh fuck," she pants, leaning her head against my shoulder, her hips bucking faster.

"You're so fucking wet for me, baby." I add yet another finger, and she cries out.

"Please."

"Please what?"

"Please… fuck me."

"You want me to stop what I'm doing?" I ask, slowly dragging my fingers back.

She whimpers, and I plunge them in again, pumping them hard and fast while she bucks against me.

"Oh fuck, oh fuck, oh fuck."

"Come on, baby." I nibble her earlobe, then kiss down her neck, all the while fucking her with my hand.

Her whimpers grow frantic, and her legs tense around me, squeezing me tight as she cries out, "Fuck!" Her hips seize, and I keep up the momentum with my hand, letting her ride it out until she leans back, her eyes dark. "Fuck me," she growls.

"With fucking pleasure." I stomp through to the living room with her still wrapped in my arms. Laying her on the couch, I step back to unbuckle my belt and toss it aside. I shuck my jeans off, kicking them across the room before dropping to my knees in front of Barb. Taking hold of her knees, I drag her to the edge of the couch, her legs draped over my shoulders. Catching her eye, I hold her gaze while I slowly ease inside her, until I'm almost in to the hilt, then I pull back and slam in, again and again, until she's writhing beneath me.

She pulls her thighs together, balancing them on one shoulder, and crossing her feet at the top. She's so fucking tight, I don't know how much longer I can hold out.

I grab hold of her legs with one hand, and the other I slide up to her throat. She tilts her head back, but keeps her eyes fixed on mine as I press down.

Her pussy clenches tight around me, and I know she's on the edge again. I pick up the pace, thrusting harder and faster until she comes apart around me. I let loose, slamming in to the very hilt, my cock throbbing in time with her.

Collapsing onto her, I listen to her heart racing beneath my ear and let out a long breath. "Fuck, babe, I needed that."

She lets out a throaty laugh. "I was only gone two nights." Her fingers thread through my hair, massaging my scalp.

I sigh. "Two nights too long."

"Rough weekend?" she asks.

"You could say that."

"Mine wasn't exactly smooth sailing either."

I raise my head, planting a kiss to the base of her throat. "Wanna talk about it?"

She snorts. "Not particularly."

"Good. Me neither." I push her top up, exposing her breasts. "I have much more pressing matters to attend to."

CHAPTER TWENTY-TWO

BARB

We pull up outside Mama K's place to find my father's car parked out front, along with Juanita's and another I'm not familiar with.

"I see Dad didn't waste any time taking Mama K up on the offer of a coffee anytime." I turn to Matiu with a raised brow, and he shrugs.

"She makes a mean coffee, and everyone likes her. I don't know why you're so surprised."

I follow him up the path. "I mean, I thought he was hanging out with you this weekend, but whatever."

He stops with one foot on the bottom step, turning to face me. "He has been hanging out with me. At the clubhouse for drinks. Then I introduced him to Aldrin and he took him for a look around his cars." He shrugs again. "Shiiit, woman, he's a big boy. He don't need me holding his hand every minute." He shakes his head, but there's a smile on his lips.

Before we can make it up the steps though, the door flies open, and Dad pulls to a stop when he sees us.

"Oh! I didn't know you were back, pumpkin." He laughs nervously, and there's a weird expression on his face. Like he's been caught doing something he shouldn't.

"Ah, surprise," I say, holding my hands up in front of me.

"I, um." He pulls the door closed behind him, leaving us all standing far too close to one another. I take a step back behind Matiu so he has space to pass.

"Everything okay?" I ask as his eyes dart back and forth between the two of us.

"Everything is hunky dory." He touches his finger to his thumb in the universal sign of 'okay' and steps past us.

"You sure?" Matiu levels him with a stare, his arms folded across his chest.

Dad stutters as he nods then leans in to give me a kiss on the cheek. "I've got to get going." He rests his hand on my shoulder. "I'm not leaving for a few more hours if you need me." He gives Matiu a side-long look then darts down the path to his car.

"That was weird," I say, watching him clamber in and pull away from the curb.

"You don't think he and Ma…" He lets his voice fade off and scrunches his nose.

"What? You think they shacked up?" I bark out a laugh. "Not a chance in hell."

"What's that supposed to mean?"

"I just don't think they're each other's types."

"Ma is a catch. He'd be lucky to have her after your mother."

I quirk a brow, folding my arms slowly across my chest. "Well, which is it? You want there to be something between them or not? Because I got the feeling you didn't from that look on your face. So did Dad." I wave my hand at the empty parking space out front. "Clearly."

"That's not… I like your dad, I do, but that's a little too close to home." He shudders. "It's like incest or something."

I snort. "That's not how that works, babe."

"I know it's not, but it *feels* like it is. You know what I mean."

I get it. My dad and his mum would be all kinds of weird. "Yeah, I do, but I don't know. My dad isn't exactly a ladies' man. He's only ever been with my mum. I don't think he'd be so quick to jump into anything else. Pretty sure he's still hoping she'll take him back."

"I think he's shit outta luck there."

"No shit, Sherlock." I roll my eyes. "Are we going in or we just gonna sit out here all day?"

He stomps up the steps, kicking his boots off at the top before pushing the door open. "Hey, Ma," he calls as he saunters down the hall and into the lounge.

145

I'm following so close behind that I don't register he's stopped until I walk right into him.

"What the?" I pull up, rubbing my nose and giving him the stink eye.

"Son," Mama K says at the same time as Juanita says, "Matiu." They look guilty as sin, and I can see why. Standing between them is Anaru.

CHAPTER TWENTY-THREE

MATIU

I feel like I've walked into an alternate reality, where I've come face-to-face with a different version of myself. This man standing in Ma's lounge looks just like me, and everyone looks like they're about to shit their pants. What the fuck have I walked in on here?

"What's going on?" I ask, and behind me, Barb slides her hand into mine, giving it a squeeze. I move aside so she can come through the door too, but I'm not moving any further than that. It's a struggle to get my mind to work, let alone my body.

"Ah, hi." The guy steps forward, his hand outstretched. "I'm Anaru." He nods at Barb. "Barb."

"Hey, Anaru."

My head flicks around to her so quick it gives me whiplash. "You know this guy?"

"We've met." We'll be talking about that later.

"Yeah, ah, when I met Barb the other night and we got to chatting, I knew I had to come here and see for myself." He waves two fingers between the two of us. "You may have noticed we look alike?"

"I have eyes, so yeah." I look to Ma, who's wringing her hands together. "What is this?"

"Matiu," Juanita starts, patting the seat beside her. "Why don't you come and sit down?"

I shake my head. "I'm good here, thanks."

"Look, there's no easy way to say this, so I'm just going to throw it out there." Anaru glances back at Juanita and Ma, who reach out and clutch hands. "I think I might be your father."

I knew what he was going to say before he said it, but it still throws me for a six. All my life I've wanted a father, someone to look up to, to show me how to be a man, teach me things Ma couldn't. I wished so hard for it every birthday that I'd get to meet him one day, and now that I'm faced with him, I can't even form a fucking sentence.

"I know this is a lot to take in. Believe me, I was thrown by it too. I had no idea you even existed until two nights ago, and even then I wasn't certain. But looking at you in the flesh... there's no question." Anaru rakes a hand through his hair. "I'm not about to pretend I know the first thing about being a father, and I don't for a second think you need me stepping in and giving you advice. You seem to be doing alright for yourself." He gestures to Barb. "But, if you're open to it, I'd like to get to know you."

Beside me, Barb squeezes my hand again, but I still can't get any words to come out of my mouth. What do you say to a man claiming to be your father after 23 years?

Ma clears her throat. "Matiu, you okay?"

I snap my eyes to hers. "Did you know?"

She shakes her head. "I had no idea until about an hour ago." Her gaze shifts to Juanita, who's eyes glisten with tears.

"I'm so sorry, Matiu." She drops her head into her hands.

"I don't…" I swallow, turning back to Anaru. "How?"

"I used to come here every summer, doing seasonal work. The last time I was here, I met someone, and we started hanging out a lot over the time I was here. Then one day, out of the blue, she took off. No goodbye, not a word." He lets out a sigh. "I was devastated. When I moved onto the next place, I decided I wouldn't come back here again, and I didn't… until last night."

"Um, why does that make you Matiu's father? Who is this mysterious woman, and where the hell is she?" Barb pipes up, asking the very same question I had on my mind. If he's my father, then who is my mother? And why are Ma and Nita so sure of it?

"Because," Juanita says, "your mother… is Sarah."

149

"Who's Sarah?" Barb asks, but I already know. It makes so much sense now why she's been such a big part of my life. Not just because Ma helped her out, but because she's my family. My grandmother.

"My daughter." Juanita sniffles. "You have to understand. She was finally clean, and then she was spending every waking moment with Anaru and... things began to change. She was throwing up every day, barely eating, moody. I thought..." She shakes her head, her lip trembling. "I thought she was using again. I confronted her, and she denied it. The next morning she was gone, like Anaru said."

"So you've known this whole time?" Barb asks, incredulously. "Why didn't you say anything? Jesus, you had to know how much this would mean to him."

"I swear, I didn't know at first. But as you grew older, I could see the resemblance to Anaru, but I didn't know what to do about it. I had no way of contacting him. I only knew his first name." She pauses, taking in a shaky breath. "And I didn't want to believe Sarah was capable of abandoning a child."

"So you just lied to me this whole time?" I seethe, my eyes stinging with tears that I blink away. "I've spent my life not knowing who I really am, and you could've told me years ago!"

"Hey, mate." Anaru steps into my line of sight, his hands up in a placating manner. "Let's calm it down, okay?"

"Move."

"Look, everyone's in high emotion right now, how about we take a break? Cool off a bit?"

"You don't get to come in here and make decisions for me. I have questions that need answers, and she's going to give them to me."

"I get it, man, I do. But look at her. You're scaring her. Everyone's upset."

"Ha!" That's a fucking understatement. "The only person who has a right to be upset right now, is me. It's me who grew up feeling like I didn't fit in anywhere, like I wasn't wanted, when all along, *she* knew where I belonged and didn't say a fucking word." I turn to Juanita. "I actually respected you. I went into bat for you with Jeri, and all this time, you've been keeping secrets. How could you keep this from me?" My voice breaks, and before she can answer, I shove past Barb and out the door. I don't bother waiting for her, because right now, I'm not so keen on her either.

Chapter Twenty-Four

Barb

"Jesus, guys. A little heads up would've been nice," I say to the room. I know better than to go after him. When Matiu gets like this, it's better to leave him be. He'll calm down and talk when he's ready, and whenever that is, I'll be there to listen.

Mama K stands abruptly. "If I'd known you were coming around…" She shakes her head, gathering the coffee mugs from the table with a sigh. "I wouldn't have known what to say then either."

"It's a lot to throw on someone. I had all night to think about it before I decided to come here and find out for myself, and I'm still trying to wrap my head around it. I have a son." Anaru takes the coffee mugs from Mama K's hand and suggests she sit back down. She's pale and shaking, and I can't imagine how hard this must be for her.

"Have you spoken to Sarah? Has she confirmed this?" I press, even though there's no denying the similarities between them.

Juanita chews her lip, nodding her head. "Yes." It's barely a whisper. "There was a letter. Matiu would've been about five at the time."

Mama K stiffens. "And you didn't tell me?"

"I'm sorry, I didn't know what to do, and I haven't heard from her since. I never, for a second, would've thought she'd do such a thing, abandoning her child like that, but she did, and I have to live with that." Her gaze turns to Anaru as he comes back through from the kitchen. "And if there was ever any doubt about the father, there isn't now. There's no denying the resemblance, especially now I see you in the flesh again. It was so long ago." She takes a gulping breath. "I swear I tried again to find her when I received the letter but came up empty. She clearly doesn't want to be found."

"Why would she leave him here with Mama K though? Why not with you?"

"Believe me, I've wondered that myself over the years – not that he didn't have the best here with you, Celeste. He was lucky to have a strong woman like you raising him." She huffs out a breath, rubbing a hand across her forehead. "Maybe she believed I wasn't the right person to raise a child. She didn't think much of my parenting." A sob breaks free, and Mama K lets out a sigh.

"Don't go blaming yourself, Nita. You know as well as I do how much of a handful that child of yours

153

was. There's not a woman alive who could've done a better job than what you did for her." Mama K reaches across and grabs her friend's hand. "You were a good mother."

Juanita scoffs. "I'm a mother who has no idea where her child is. I'd hardly say that's a recipe for a good mother."

I don't bother trying to stroke her ego with praise. She doesn't get to play the martyr here. Matiu is the one who missed out on a family.

"And you?" I turn to Anaru instead. "What do you want out of this? You could've forgotten about it and lived in blissful ignorance, and he would never have known. Why'd you come here and upend his world?"

"I didn't mean to cause him any pain, and I don't want anything but to get to know him, and you. We're family. I know it's late in the picture, but we can still be involved in each other's lives. And I know, if he's open to it, there's a whole lot more family out there who will want to be involved too. If he'll agree to it, that is."

Not having a father has framed who Matiu is. I think it's why he joined the Hellhounds, to have that connection he'd been missing. It's like a family unit where they all look out for each other. Yeah, he's got Mama K and Juanita, but the Hellhounds have been there for him like a second home. They helped raise him into the man he is today.

"If you really want to do this, I'll talk to him. But you have to be all in. He doesn't need someone coming into his life who's going to leave when life gets in the way, okay? Last year he lost someone he looked up to. Tony was like a father figure to him, and I don't know if he could take it if you came into his life and then walked out again."

"I understand that, and I'm not trying to turn his life upside down. I'm not planning on going anywhere, except back home, but it's close enough we can visit. Hell, if I can convince Shaz, maybe we could move here to be closer to him. I don't know."

"You would uproot your life to move closer to your adult son you've only just found out about?"

"Of course I would. He's my blood. We're whanau."

I nod, blinking back the tears threatening to fall. "Okay then. I'll talk to him. See if I can get him to come around to it, alright? But I can't make any promises. This is a lot."

"I know, and I'm sorry. I never meant to spring it on him like this. We were discussing how best to approach it when you walked in."

"That explains why Dad was acting so weird on the way out." I snort, happy for the break in tension. "Matiu thought he might've had the hots for you, Mama K."

That gets a smile out of her. "Lord, that boy will be the death of me. Anytime I'm friendly with a man, he thinks there's something going on. It took me weeks to convince him there was nothing between me and the postman, all because I would say hi every time he passed by." She shakes her head. "He's always been so protective of me." Her eyes well up, and she reaches for a tissue. "Excuse me," she says, dabbing at her eyes.

"That's not gonna change, Celeste. Just because he knows where he's from, doesn't mean he's going to forget where his home is." Juanita wraps her arms around Mama K, squeezing her tight. "He's always known you weren't his biological mother, and he's loved you all the same, right?"

Mama K sniffs and nods.

"That's not about to change because he's suddenly got a dad and grandmother."

"Absolutely not," Anaru adds. "We're all in this together. Whanau is whanau, however it comes together."

CHAPTER TWENTY-FIVE

MATIU

I didn't plan on coming here, I was on autopilot, but now that I see the Hellhounds insignia on the door, a sense of calm falls over me. It's like the knot in my shoulders just disappears into nothing as I step through the door and up the stairs.

I knock on the door then let myself in. Sam is in the kitchen making coffee, and she turns to me with a warm smile. "Hey, Matiu." I must look a mess because her smile turns into a frown, and she rushes towards me. "What's wrong? Is it Barb?"

"No, no." I reach around to scratch the back of my neck. "She's fine. I just..." I glance around the room. "Is Jeri here? I really need to talk to him."

She folds her arms across her chest. "Is this about that brothel you're trying to wrangle the Hellhounds into?"

"He told you about that, huh?"

She raises her brow. "Of course he did. Did you run it past Barb?"

"I mentioned it."

"Mmmhmm." She eyes me.

"It's not as bad as it sounds. I'm just trying to help out a..." A what? Nita has always been a friend. A sort of surrogate aunt, I suppose. But she's more than that now, isn't she? She's my grandmother. My *real* family.

I clear my throat. "I just wanted to help Nita fix things." I shrug. "I thought it was a good idea."

Her face softens, and she reaches out, running her hand down my arm. "She's lucky to have you looking out for her." Her fingers flex, giving me a squeeze before stepping into the hall. "Jericho, Matiu's here."

"The hell does he want?" he calls back, swinging their bedroom door open.

"Coffee?" Sam asks, holding a mug in the air as she pads back into the kitchen.

"I think I need something a lot stronger than that."

"Ooh, it's one of those conversations, is it?" She grimaces, handing Jeri his mug and scooting past him. "Are you sure it's not..." She holds up her hands.

"Never mind. It's none of my business. I'll leave you boys to it."

"Thanks."

She stops in the doorway. "And, for the record, it is a good idea. I was just playing with you." She smiles, then turns and makes her way down the hall.

"What's this all about?" Jeri nods towards the living area, and I follow. "You look like shit."

"Shiiit, way to kick a man when he's down." But weirdly, it has the opposite effect. This right here is my family. This is what I know. Where everything feels right.

"I call it as I see it." He leans back, resting his arm across the back of the couch. "Barb finally come to her senses and call the wedding off?"

"Fuck off, old man."

"Something's clearly bothering you though, so what is it?"

I let out a long shaky breath. Hot tears prick my eyes, and I blink them away before they can fall.

"Jesus, bro, what is it?" Jeri leans forward, his elbows braced on his knees. "Talk to me."

"My... *Dad* is in town." I swallow the lump lodged in my throat.

"Your... what?"

"Yeah. You heard right."

"Fuck." He scrubs a hand across his jaw. "I didn't know... I mean, I knew you *had* one, but I didn't think you knew who it was."

"I didn't. He showed up today. Apparently he met Barb in Hanmer?" I shrug. "I don't know, man. It's fucking weird and I'm trippin' out."

"That's..."

"Yeah."

"And you're here with me instead of with him." He lets his words hang in the air, like I should feel obligated to this guy I've never met until today. Like I should be playing happy families or some shit.

"Yeah, I am." I hold his gaze. "I couldn't be in that room another second." Pushing up off the chair, I stalk to the other side of the room and stare out the window. "She knew this whole time and didn't say anything."

"Who? Barb?"

"No, though she obviously knew something. But I mean Juanita. She knew who my parents were, and she said nothing. Not a damn thing."

"Hold up. I'm confused. What does Juanita have to do with this?"

I laugh, but there's no humour in it. "That's the thing I can't wrap my head around." Tilting my head back, I pinch the bridge of my nose. "Turns out she's been a huge part of my life because she feels guilty or some shit."

"I don't follow."

"Her daughter, Sarah? She's my mother. But instead of raising me herself, she decided to dump and run. Guess a baby cramps the style of a junkie." I laugh again, only this time it leaves a bitter taste in my mouth. "I don't know how I didn't figure it out sooner.

I mean, why else would she be at every birthday and Christmas? Why else would she be so present in the life of her friend's kid? People don't just do that without reason."

"Mate, give her some credit. Only yesterday you were ready to jump to her rescue, and now you're acting like she's done you dirty all these years, but really, what has she done? You said yourself she's been at every family event. She's been present in your life. That's more than a lot of people can say."

"But it's all been a lie."

"Has it though? You didn't know she was 'officially' family, but haven't you always treated each other that way? What's the difference?"

"Dude, who's side are you on? She lied to me."

"I'm not on anyone's side here, but not telling you something and lying are two very different things. I think you're missing the point here, bro."

"Yeah? And what's that?"

"She loves you. If she didn't, she wouldn't have been so involved. Maybe, and I'm just throwing this out there, but maybe she had her reasons. Like maybe you'd throw a hissy fit like the one you're throwing right now." He folds his arms and quirks a brow at me. "Think about it, bro, if she had told you when you were younger, how would it have made you feel? What could you have done about it?"

I huff out a breath. "Nothing, I guess."

"Right, so maybe she was trying to save you the hurt of knowing and thinking that you weren't..." He winces, waving a hand through the air. "… wanted, for lack of a better word."

"I spent my whole life feeling that way, old man. Like a piece of shit no one wants."

"Mate, you know that's not true." He stands, coming to stand at the window beside me. "You think Mama K raised you as her own out of boredom or obligation? That woman loves you as if she's the one who carried you nine months."

"She found me on her doorstep. She didn't have much choice in the matter."

Jericho grabs my shoulder and turns me to face him. "That's bullshit and you know it. She didn't have to raise you, she *chose* to. She could've just as easily handed you to the authorities, but she adopted you and took you in."

He's right, and I know it.

"Stop feeling sorry for yourself and realise how bloody lucky you are to have been raised by two strong women who would do just about anything for you. Having parents isn't always all it's cracked up to be, believe me. And, if I'm not mistaken, you just walked out on the one who's trying to make up for lost time. Don't piss that away."

"Jeri, I didn't…"

He holds his hand up. "I know you didn't. But you need a reality check right now. I had a father growing up, and he was a piece of shit. He's the reason I find it hard to trust, and why I have no family left except for Sam and you guys. But you've had a family this whole time, one that might not be your typical

162

family, but a family all the same, and one that loves you. I would give anything to have my family back. Anything."

I swallow the lump in my throat. When I look at it from his perspective, yeah, I'm acting like a prize pussy right now. Given what he went through, I've got nothing to complain about.

"Okay, yeah. You're right."

"I know I am. That's why I wear the vest that says president, and you don't."

CHAPTER TWENTY-SIX

BARB

By the time Matiu pulls into the drive, I'm passed the worried girlfriend stage and onto the angry fiancé one. I get that this is a lot to take in, but it's nearing nine at night, and I've not heard a word from him since he walked out of Mama K's hours ago.

"Hey," he says as he walks in the door and takes a seat. No apology, nothing.

"Your dinner is on the table. It's cold. I've already eaten." My foot bounces against the coffee table until I force it still.

Matiu groans, leaning his head back to rest on the chair, his eyes scrunched closed. "Not you too. Jeri's already ripped me a new one."

I snort at that. I can always count on Jericho Lawson to get Matiu to pull his head in. Pushing up to stand, I walk towards the kitchen to retrieve his plate, but he stops me with his hand on my thigh. His fingers curl into me, holding me in place.

"Why didn't you tell me about Anaru?"

"When was I meant to tell you? Before or after you ripped my clothes off? I didn't exactly have time." I fold my arms across my chest, and he levels me with a stare.

"You could've warned me."

I glare right back. "I could've warned you that I met some guy who looked like you? Jesus, Matiu, I get that you're upset or whatever, but don't turn your anger on me."

His fingers flex against my thigh and he squeezes his eyes closed again, letting out a long breath. "Sorry. I'm being a prick. It's been a fucked up day."

I don't say anything, just stand there, looking away from him.

"I'm sorry I stormed out too."

All the air huffs out of me. "I get why you did, but you could've messaged. It's been hours." Jesus, I sound like one of those girls who need to keep tabs on their man 24/7. We're not like that; we don't live in each other's pockets, but this is different. He was angry, and when people are angry, especially people like Matiu, they do stupid shit that get them into trouble.

"I know. I just needed to think things through, and Jeri helped put things in perspective. Made me see straight."

"You just..." *Accused me of keeping secrets* I want to say, but I don't. "Whatever." My tone is clipped, and I don't even know why. It's not like I don't know what a bombshell this was for him. *God, I need to loosen up.*

He sighs. "You're still mad though." He looks so dejected, like the day has taken everything out of him. He doesn't need me adding to it.

"I'm not mad," I say. "I'm just… disappointed." The corners of my lips quirk up and he gives me the side eye.

"Fuck you." He yanks me onto his lap, wrapping his arms around me. "I thought you were really pissed."

"I was, but I'm not a total bitch, you know. I *do* understand why you reacted the way you did. But would it kill you to let me know you're okay?"

"You worried about me, babe?"

"Pssh, hardly." I curl into his side, nuzzling my face in the crook of his neck. His whiskers scratch against my face. "I've only been gone a few days, what's the deal with this. You growing it?" I scrub my hand over the thick black hair. "Because I think I liked it better when you were clean shaven."

"Yeah?" He tilts his head this way and that. "I thought you liked beards?"

"Oh, I do. And you look hot, but I miss the smooth face. Plus, the beard rash is nasty." I squeeze my thighs together, and he swats my behind.

"I didn't hear any complaints this afternoon."

"You don't interrupt an artist at work. The pain was worth it at the time, but the aftereffects aren't as fun."

"Aww, you need me to kiss it better?" He tugs at my waistband, but I swat him away.

"Not a chance."

"Wait, you're serious?" He strokes his chin. "You want me to lose it?"

I trail a finger across his jaw. "I do."

"Be right back." With his hands firmly on my hips, he hoists me from his lap.

I laugh. "I didn't mean right this second."

But he's already at the bathroom door. "You'd better be naked and waiting when I get back."

I grin. He's back. The cocky, sure-of-himself man I love so fucking much.

HELLHOUNDS MC

CHAPTER TWENTY-SEVEN

MATIU

Before I can even think of facing Anaru again, I need to square things up with Nita. I'm ashamed of the way I acted yesterday. Jeri was right, no matter what happened in the past, Nita has always been there for me, she's always stood by me, and I shat on that when I called her a liar. I have to make things right.

When I pull up outside her place, there are unfamiliar cars in her drive, and I'm instantly on edge. I don't need any more surprises coming out of the woodwork right now. I set my helmet on the back of my bike and head up the path to the front door.

The sound of raised voices comes from inside, and I dial Jeri then tuck the phone in my back pocket. I don't bother knocking, just barge on through the door.

"Nita? Everything okay?" I call out as I stride through the house in search of her.

"Matiu?" Is that relief in her voice? Who the fuck is here with her?

"The fuck are you doing here?" A gruff voice demands as none other than Curtis Montgomery steps out from the kitchen. His stance is wide, one hand reaching behind his back.

Holding my hands up, I stop still, keeping an eye on the hand I can't see.

"I don't want any trouble. I'm just here to see Juanita is all." There's movement behind him, but I can't tell who it is. "Nita, you okay?"

There's a groan and then her voice, small and unlike I've ever heard it before. "Yes, I'm fine."

My eyes narrow. "What have you done to her?"

"We're just having a little business chat, aren't we, *Nita*?" He glances behind, giving me a glimpse of her sitting at the table, and Murphy standing behind her with his hands firmly on her shoulders.

"Didn't she tell you? There is no business. The deal is off."

"The deal ain't off unless I say it's off." Curtis runs a tongue along his top teeth. "And Nita here knows that. She just needed reminding. Didn't you, sweetheart?"

Murphy's hands tighten on her shoulders, and she lets out a squeak before nodding. "Mmhmm."

169

"So your little plan to takeover is bust, mate. You can just mosey on outta here and let us finish our little chat."

"I'm not going anywhere."

There's the unmistakable sound of a gun cocking. "I got something here says otherwise."

Nita's eyes widen. "Matiu, it's okay. I'm okay." Her eyes flick between Curtis's hand and me.

"You're not okay, and I'm not leaving you alone with them."

"Please, I can sort this out. I can make it right." Tears course down her cheeks. "You need to go."

"You heard the lady. Off you fuck. Let the men take care of business." He runs his tongue along his teeth again, this time grabbing his cock at the same time. "I think I can feel us a deal coming on."

"Don't you fucking touch her." With my hands balled into fists, I make to move towards him, but he draws the gun, aiming at Nita's head.

"Or what?" He cocks his head. "Seems to me you're not the one should be making threats, boy."

"Please, Matiu. I can do this. It's okay." Juanita reaches her shaking fingers to the buttons of her shirt and begins undoing them. "Please, just go."

"You don't have to do this."

Curtis swings the gun in my direction. "You're the one who put the idea in her head she should back out, and that, my friend, is a huge fucking deal. One that's going to cost me a lot of money, so either she gets fucked, or you do. Only difference is, she'll still be

170

able to walk away after." He sniggers. "Well... maybe not straight away."

Juanita raises her chin defiantly. "I've made a lot of mistakes in my life, and I'm not about to make you pay for another one. I got us into this, I'll get us out." She pulls her lip between her teeth as fresh tears brim. "I need you to turn around and walk away. You can't see me like this. Please."

"Nita, no."

"Yes."

The glint of the gun pointed at me draws my attention. "You heard the lady." He nods towards the door. "Get out."

"Not. A. Chance. You fucking touch her and I'll kill you." I take a step forward, knowing this may be the last thing I ever do and hoping like fuck Barb can forgive me for leaving her. I was a fool to think Nita was anything but family.

There's an explosion behind me and a flash in front of my eyes before searing pain hits my shoulder and I drop to the floor.

"Oh fuck!" Someone grabs me under my other arm and drags me towards the door, as fire burns through my shoulder. Jeri and Stubbs run past, towards the kitchen. Another shot is fired, voices yelling, but I'm already halfway out the door and can't see what's going on. A scuffle, another shot, then silence.

"Leave me! Nita!" I yell. "Nita, are you okay?"

Sirens blare in the distance, but all I can think is that they're too late. Someone's not walking out of there alive.

171

CHAPTER TWENTY-EIGHT

BARB

"You ready for this?" I ask as we approach the door. It's only been a week since Matiu was shot in this very house, and I know I wouldn't be anywhere near the place so soon after if it'd been me. Thankfully the bullet went straight through and, though he's still in a sling, the recovery hasn't been too bad so far. He was only in overnight, and with a bit of physio, he should be back on his feet again. Unlike poor Stubbs. He didn't fare quite so well, with a bullet to the foot. Took three of his toes clean off, and the boys have been giving him hell. Not only does he have stubs for fingers, he now has stubs for toes as well. How unlucky can you be? Though, I guess, in the grand scheme of things, he's lucky it hadn't been any higher and the damage was minimal, relatively speaking. If Holden hadn't come in through the back door and tackled Curtis from behind, it could've been much worse.

Now Stubbs is laid up in hospital, with all the nurses wrapped around his little finger, but he promises he'll be out by the wedding next weekend. He bloody better be, because I'm not doing it twice.

Matiu lets out a slow breath, staring up at the house. "I guess this is it."

I link my fingers through his, squeezing. "It'll be fine. How many of them can there be?"

The door swings open and Mama K steps out. "There you are." She makes her way down the steps to us, giving Matiu a peck on the cheek and taking hold of my hand. "How is it today?"

Matiu shrugs with his good shoulder. "Same shit, different day."

Mama K tuts, but I can tell she's just happy to see him on his feet. We were all shaken when Jeri called us from the hospital and gave us the lowdown. I honestly didn't know what to expect, especially after the last time the Hellhounds were involved in a shootout. Tony's memory still lingers in the clubroom, and no one is ready for there to be another casualty.

"They're all out back, waiting for you. Come on." She beckons us to follow.

Once inside, the bustle of voices and music carries through from out the ranch slider leading to the backyard. It sounds like a lot more than 'just a few' people, like Anaru said it would be. I glance at Matiu, who suddenly looks pale as a ghost.

"You okay?"

"Yeah, just…" He swallows, sucking in another deep breath and tipping his head back. He closes his eyes. "Shiiiiit."

"What is it?"

He meets my gaze, and I'm taken aback by the glassy look to them. He's choked up. "This is my family. I've never… I've never had that before." He glances at Mama K. "I mean, not like this." He waves his hand towards the door. "I don't even know what I'm doing."

Mama K sniffs, swiping a finger beneath her eye to clear away the tears brimming. "Baby boy, you know I love you, and that's never going to change. But out there is a whole bunch of people who are dying to meet you and get to know you. You don't have to do anything but be yourself, you'll see. They're going to love you."

She steps through the door and a hush falls over the group. Someone turns the music down, and all that's left are the heavy footfalls climbing up onto the deck.

"You've got this," I whisper, giving his hand one last squeeze before nudging him through the door.

Anaru greets him with an outstretched hand, which Matiu accepts. They pull into each other, pressing their foreheads and noses together in a hongi. All around them people are sobbing and hugging each other. It's beautiful.

When they part, Anaru turns to face the crowd of at least two dozen people with a grin. "Guys, this is Matiu. My son."

The sobbing grows louder, and people gather in close, hands reaching towards them both. I stay behind Matiu, letting him have this moment, and, if I'm honest, hiding my own tearstained face from view.

"And this—" Anaru waves at the crowd, "—is your whanau." He gestures to the two couples closest. "This is my oldest brother, Wiremu, and his wife Arana. My younger brother, Nikau, and his wife Eileen." He points to another group behind them. "My big sister, Maia, her partner Jess, and their new bubba Cleo. That's Ari and her husband Jordan." He stops, looking sheepish. "And you're probably not going to remember any of that, are you?" He chuckles.

"I think I've forgotten my own name at this point." Matiu scratches a hand down his jaw.

"Kia ora, Matiu." Wiremu takes his hand, leaning in for a hongi. "This is probably a bit much, eh? Bet you weren't expecting all these fellas to show up."

Matiu snorts. "Shiiiiit, mate, you got that right."

Wiremu laughs, deep and throaty. "You'll get used to us all."

"Yeah, and then he'll be sick of the sight of us!" Arana bustles in to give him a kiss on the cheek. "Welcome to the whanau, hon."

"Ai," Wiremu says. "You'll have to come back home with us sometime, see the marae. Get to know your roots."

"Geez, man, give him some air to breathe." Nikau rolls his eyes. "Let him get used to the fact he's got an instant family before you start up with that stuff." To Matiu, he says, "Just tell him to piss off or he'll keep going. Doesn't know when to shut-up, eh, Anaru?"

He snickers. "He's not wrong. Once he gets started, there's no stopping him."

Someone taps on my shoulder, and before I've even turned fully, they're introducing themselves.

"Oh my God, hi, I'm Greg, and this is Roimata." A staunch woman with long jet-black hair and blonde highlights pulls me in for a hug, while Greg, who has the most luscious curls I'm actually jealous, grabs hold of Matiu's arm. "As soon as Uncle said he had a son, I was like get outta here, I *have* to meet him! So we jumped on the first flight we could, eh cuz?"

"Hell yeah. There was no chance we'd miss coming out to meet you guys." Roimata's dark eyes glisten. "I can't even believe it, eh. Boom, just like that, another cousin."

"And you two are getting married soon, right?" Greg bounces on his toes, hands clasped together. "I love that for you."

"Next week, if he can fit into his suit." I eye Matiu's sling with a smirk.

"Suit? Who said anything about a suit? I can fit my leathers over this, piece of piss."

"Ooh, kinky." Greg chuckles, and Matiu snorts.

"Not that kind of leather, bro. I'm a Hellhound." He taps the patch on his vest. "But if Barb wanted to sport something kinky and leather, I wouldn't say no."

176

I backhand his good arm. "That's for after the wedding, not during."

"I like her." Roimata grins, pointing at me.

Greg sighs wistfully. "I love weddings."

"You just like dressing up." Roimata pokes her tongue between her teeth, and Greg waves a dismissive hand, complete with painted nails.

"Of course I do, but it's more than that. It's the romance of it. Two people finding each other and choosing to be together. It's bea-*utiful*." He clasps his hands together. "Don't you think?"

"You guys want to come?" I ask. "I mean, I don't know how long you're here for, but if you want to—" I don't get to finish my sentence before Greg grabs me by the arms and crushes me to him.

"Oh my God, are you serious? Yes! A thousand times yes!" He turns to the group nearest. "Everyone, we're going to a wedding!"

"Shiiiiit," Matiu says under his breath, "we're gonna need a bigger venue."

"Welcome to the whanau, cuz." Roimata laughs, watching Greg run around inviting everyone. "You're never getting rid of us now."

CHAPTER TWENTY-NINE

MATIU

The past few days have been unreal. I had no idea having a family this size would be so exhausting, but it is. I think I'm finally getting my head wrapped around who's who and where they fit in, but it's a lot. A hell of a lot.

Aside from Greg and Roimata, there are another ten cousins. Roimata has her own kids too, and so does Molly, so I guess they're like my second cousins or something. I don't know. All I know is there's a lot of them, and I'm one of them now too.

Barb is, and always will be, my ride or die. She's my fucking world. But meeting the family has filled something I didn't even know needed filling. It's like there was this huge chunk of me missing, and now I feel whole. Like I belong.

Of course, they'll all go back up north eventually, and I'll be back to normal life here, but just knowing they're there... it's something else.

Here, though, in the other place I belong, Jeri takes his seat at the head of the table with Sam pulling up a chair beside him. Barb is beside me, and Darcy and Cami take up seats either side of Holden. Stubbs is, as always, by Jeri's side, and Zeb is at the other end of the table. The only one missing is Cassian, and there's no surprise there. The kid has been so flighty since Jodi started toying with him. The sooner he wises up and gets rid of her, the better.

There's a knock on the door, and Juanita pokes her head in. Jeri waves her in, and she takes a seat beside Barb.

"Okay, now that we're all out of the woods and back on our feet—" he glances at Stubbs with a grin, "—as much as we can be, we need to discuss this new business venture." He gestures around the room. "Ladies, we've brought you in on this because we want your input. You need something fixed? We're on it. Need security? We're there. But when it comes to running a business like this—" he spreads his hands out, palms up, "—we're clueless."

I eye Zeb. "I don't know, man, I think Zeb's been to a few of these establishments over the years. He probably knows a thing or two. Right, bro?" I grin at him, and he flips me the bird.

"Pssh, whatever." He leans back in his seat, hands linking behind his head. "I got plenty of game without having to pay for it."

"Tell that to your Pornhub subscription." Cami snickers.

"Now why would I need Pornhub when I've got a pretty thing like you to look at, darlin'?" he asks, waggling his brows at her. I've got to give it to him, he's a tryer. Dude hasn't given up since he first laid eyes on Cami.

She rolls her eyes, poking her finger in her mouth and pretending to gag.

"You love it." Zeb winks, rocking back on his chair.

"Jesus Christ, you lot. Can we get on track please?"

Zeb salutes. "Sorry, boss."

"Right, we have a building lined up already, don't we, Juanita?"

She nods. "That's right. It's a few blocks down from here in the old youth hostel. It was sitting empty, so council was happy for me to utilise it. Curtis had nothing to do with the acquisition, no name on leases or anything. That's what he came to see me about…" Her voice trails off, and she swallows, clasping her hands together on the table, staring at them a beat. "I haven't thanked you for what you did that day."

Jeri holds his hand up. "No thanks necessary. We're just glad we could get there before things got out of hand."

She nods. "Still. If you hadn't shown up when you did…" Her voice trails off and she swallows. "It took me back to a time I'd rather forget."

"And that's exactly why we want in on this, and why we need your help with it. So this kind of shit doesn't happen."

"I know. I'm kicking myself for not doing my homework on those two. Neither of you would've been hurt if I had."

Stubbs taps his finger on the table to draw her attention. "I'd happily take another bullet if it meant those two were out of action. If this hadn't happened, Curtis wouldn't be sitting in a jail cell right now, and Murphy wouldn't be in a whole world of pain dealing with a bullet wound to the stomach, so there's some good that's come out of it."

"But… your toes…"

He shrugs. "Eh, it's not like I use them. Now I have a matching set." He holds up his stubby hand and grins.

Juanita lets out something like a half laugh, half sigh.

"What's done is done, all we can do is move forward." Jeri turns to Cami. "We thought you'd be a good fit for running the place, if you're up for it?"

Cami looks taken aback, pointing a finger at her own chest. "Me?" She glances at Holden, who nods. "Um, yeah, sure. I don't really know what I'm doing though."

"That's also where you come in, Juanita. We'd like you to oversee the business, at least in the

181

beginning. Make sure it runs smoothly, point out anything that needs changing. We want to do this right."

She nods. "I can do that."

"The boys and I will each run security in shifts, at least until we can vet some new guys." He takes a moment to look each of the women in the eye. "You okay with that?"

Barb snorts. "He strays, he knows where the door is." She quirks her brow at me, as if setting a challenge.

"Shiiiit, woman. I know what I've got at home. Lady on the streets, and a freak in the sheets." I poke my tongue out, and Holden barks out a laugh.

"She ain't no lady."

Barb folds her arms across her chest, cocking her head as she levels him with a stare.

"I mean… of course you're a lady, but you're not a *lady*, ya know?" He glances around the table to see everyone avoiding his gaze. "Guys, help me out here."

Stubbs shakes his head. "You're on your own on this one."

The door slams open behind me. "Sorry I'm late." It's Cassian, late as usual, but he's not alone. The familiar clip clop of heels walking down the corridor follows, and I inwardly groan.

I chance a glance at Barb, who has stiffened in her seat. Reaching across, I squeeze her thigh.

"What'd I miss?" Cass drags up a seat beside Zeb, and Jodi sits herself between the two of us. Closing my eyes, I suck in a deep breath through my nose. Kill me. Kill me now.

182

"I'm sorry, why is she here?" Barb spits out, hooking a thumb over her shoulder as she addresses Jeri.

"Your guess is as good as mine. Cass?" He raises a brow in question.

"What? I thought you said to bring the girls?" He looks around the table. "Everyone else has."

"This is different, dipshit," Zeb says, tilting his head in my direction. "Everyone else is long term."

"What about Cami?"

"Oh she's long term too, she just hasn't realised it yet."

He looks to Jeri. "Seriously?"

He shrugs. "We talked about this. She's a liability. We can't bring her in on our business."

Cassian's cheeks flame, his eyes narrowing. "She could help."

"We don't need *her* kind of help," Barb says.

"What's that supposed to mean?"

She swivels in her seat, her eyes like laser beams. "It means that her kind of help will only help one person; her." She drives her point home by pointing at Jodi. "Come on, Cass, surely you can see she's only here for what she can gain."

"That's not true."

"It is." Her tone shifts from anger to one of pity. "Trust me, you can do so much better than a woman who's using you to get to her ex."

"Hello? I'm right here." Jodi clicks her fingers in the air. "It's rude to talk about someone like they're not in the room."

183

Barb sucks in a breath, leaning across me. "Yeah, well it's rude to offer yourself to *my* man but that didn't stop you from trying it on, did it?"

Jodi purses her lips, tapping one manicured finger against them. "Funny, I seem to recall you doing the exact same thing when me and Matty were together."

"We were *not* together then," I clarify. "Me and Barb happened after *you* fucked your boss. Or did you forget that part?"

"Ugh." She rolls her eyes dramatically. "Why do you keep bringing that up, babe? Like I said, it didn't mean anything."

Cassian clears his throat, shifting in his seat. "Uh, babe?"

"What?"

"You called him babe."

"No I didn't."

"Yeah, you did," Cami pipes up. "We all heard it."

Jodi waves a dismissive hand. "Slip of the tongue."

"Not for the first time," Barb says under her breath, and I can't help myself, I bust out laughing.

"You know what? I don't need this." Jodi huffs, pushing up to stand. "You're all jerks." She clomps to the door then turns back, waiting for Cass to join her. "You coming?"

He frowns, his eyes darting between her and me. I give a slight shake of my head, and he turns back to the table. "No. I don't think I will."

Chapter Thirty

Barb

After all that planning, the day has finally come. I wasn't sure it would after the way things have gone down the past few weeks, but here we are. Today, I'm marrying Matiu. The guy who has made me laugh and made me cry, who has turned my whole world upside down, but in a good way. There is never a dull moment with that man, and our life is far from peaceful, but that's what I love about it. The unpredictability, the chaos. Because when it comes down to it, I know if things go south, he will be there to back me up, one hundred percent.

I wrap a towel around myself, using another to dry my hair when there's a knock at the door. "Who the hell?" I pad down the hall to where whoever is on the other side is persistently banging. "Jesus, hold on!" I unlatch the door and swing it open to find Greg, Roimata, Sam, and Jen, and each has a bag with them.

"About bloody time, chicken." Jen barges past me and through to the lounge.

"Morning, girly," Greg says, planting a kiss on my cheek as he passes.

"Bet you're regretting inviting us now, huh?" Roimata smirks.

Sam scrunches her nose and shrugs. "I tried telling them it was too early, but they were determined."

"What's all that racket?" Mum asks with a yawn. She's still in her pyjamas and wrapping a dressing gown around herself. "Oh." She stops short when she sees the lounge full of people. "You're *early*."

"You can never be too early when it comes to weddings," Jen says, placing a bag on the kitchen bench. She pulls out a tin of peaches, a punnet each of strawberries, blueberries, and raspberries, two different melons, and a bunch of bananas. "First up, we need some breakfast."

"Just a coffee and dry toast for me," Mum calls out as she pads back down the hall. "I'll just jump in the shower, make myself presentable." She mutters something else under her breath, and I can only guess as to what it was. She's never been much of a morning person. Neither of us are, to be fair.

"Sam, can you put the jug on while I get to making this fruit salad?" Jen rummages through the cupboards until she finds a bowl.

"Thank you *so* much for letting us be here." Greg perches on the edge of the couch. "Like, you have no idea how much this means to us all, right Roimata?"

She's doing a circuit of the room, checking out the photos on our walls. She stops in front of one of Matiu standing with Mama K when he was a kid. "Oh, check this out! He looks just like Uncle." She points, turning to Greg.

"Ooh, I wanna see." He jumps up, joining her. "Oh my *God*. He's so adorable."

It *is* one of my favourite photos of him. It's his first day of school and his backpack is almost bigger than he is. He has the biggest grin on his face, like he's so proud of himself. Mama K is crouched beside him with a look of pure adoration on her face.

"How long have you two been together?" Roimata turns to me with teary eyes. "Sorry." She flaps her hands and blinks rapidly. Greg reaches an arm around her, pulling her in close.

"Aww, honey," he croons. "We're all emotional right now. It's okay."

"Ugh." She swipes angrily at her tears. "It's just a photo. The wedding hasn't even started yet."

"Don't you worry, chicky, I have some great waterproof mascara you can use. No one will notice a thing." Jen slides a pile of sliced melon into the bowl and begins mixing.

"You know what, I was going to wait, but we may as well do it while I'm already crying." Roimata slips out of Greg's arms and grabs one of the bags. She pulls out a small velvet pouch. Greg clasps his hands together, bringing them in front of his mouth, his eyes alight with excitement.

"We got you something." Roimata holds the pouch over my hand, and a greenstone necklace falls into my palm.

"It's pounamu from back home."

I trail my fingers over the smooth, intricately carved stone. "It's beautiful. Thank you."

"We thought, if you didn't already have one, you could wear it today."

Jen pops up beside me. "It could be your something new."

I frown. "My what?"

"You know, something old, something new, something borrowed, something blue. It's tradition." She's staring at me like I should know this.

"Okay, but I don't have any of the other things though."

"Ooh!" Greg clutches a hand to his chest, tugging at something pinned there. "You can borrow my book pin." It's small and silver, with hearts and flowers on it, and the words *in my romance era* on it.

So not my style, but I guess we're doing this now. "Thanks."

"We could paint your nails blue too," Sam suggests.

"I guess that makes me the something old." Mum cackles, joining us in the lounge. "Or you could tuck this into your bra." She hands me a small silk handkerchief. "It was my mothers. It was my something

188

old when I married your father." She gives me a sad smile. "Hopefully it brings you better luck."

I open my mouth to speak, but nothing comes out. I don't even know what to say right now.

Jen comes to the rescue. "That's lovely, Sandra. What a great idea."

"Yeah, thanks," I manage in a husky voice.

"Now that that's sorted, I think breakfast is about ready. I've got yoghurt and croissants too." Jen unloads the remaining food onto the counter and tosses the bag aside. "Dig in."

"I'm not really that hungry." I go back to drying my hair.

"It's just the nerves. You need to eat or you'll regret it later, trust me. A wedding takes it out of you. It's a big day."

I roll my eyes, plucking a croissant from the plate and picking at it. "Fine."

Sam hands me a cup. "Coffee." As she sweeps past with two more cups, she whispers, "I have something stronger for later."

God, I could kiss her. I feel I'm going to need it.

Jen has worked wonders with my hair, pinning it up with a few curled tendrils framing my face. She clips the veil in and steps back. "Oh my gosh." Her voice is hushed, and her hands come up to her mouth. "You look gorgeous."

"Don't start or you'll get me going." I blink away tears, determined not to ruin the understated make-up Sam put on me. It wouldn't be a good look, the bride turning up with red-rimmed eyes.

"Sorry, sorry." Jen clips to the door and opens it a crack. "She's ready for you."

"About time." Mum eases through the door, stopping when she sees my reflection. "Oh, darling."

"Don't." I point at her.

She schools her features. "Right." Nodding with determination. "You ready for this?" She grabs my gown from the back of the door.

My knees feel like jelly as I stand, and there are butterflies doing laps in my stomach, but I hold my head up high. "I am."

Jen closes the door behind her, leaving the two of us alone.

Mum unhooks the gown from the hanger and holds it open for me. I slip out of my robe, tucking the handkerchief in place beneath my bra strap, and quickly step into the gown. Together, we tug the fabric into place, and she turns me back to the mirror while she buttons me up.

"You know, darling, I *am* proud of you."

I say nothing.

"And, not that my opinion matters on the subject, but you've made a good choice in Matiu."

She glances over my shoulder, catching my eye in the mirror. I quirk a brow at her.

"I'm sorry I didn't give him a chance. I was wrong to judge him before getting to know him."

I clear my throat, once again at a loss for words. "Uh, thanks?"

"What he did for his grandmother? That took guts. I can see why you love him." She places her hands on my shoulders. "And it's plain to see he's crazy about you."

"I'm crazy about him too."

She nods. "That's great. That's all I wanted for you." Her lips tremble as she smiles, fighting back tears. "Can't forget these." She pins Greg's book pin to my sleeve then helps me secure the pounamu around my neck.

Outside, there's a crash, and something bangs against the door. "Are you ready yet? We're dying to see!" Greg calls through the door.

"Shhh. Give them a minute," Jen whispers, but by the sound of it, she's also standing on the other side of the door, waiting.

I suck in a deep breath, readying myself. "Guess it's time." I give Mum the nod, and she opens the door with a flourish.

"Ta-da," she says.

Dad is front and centre, beaming at me. "Pumpkin." He takes my hands, giving them a squeeze then leaning in to plant a kiss on my cheek. "You look beautiful."

Behind him, Greg clamps both hands to his mouth. "Girl," he says between his fingers. "You look a-maze-ing." He swirls his finger in the air, and I do an

191

awkward spin for him, my trail curling around my legs. "If he doesn't marry you, I will, just sayin'." He gives me a sly grin. "Seriously, *obsessed* with this whole look."

Sam, standing to the side, smiles warmly. "Just stunning."

"More than stunning. She's a knockout." Roimata gives a nod of approval.

Jen has streaks of tears down her cheeks, and she can't seem to form words, which is a first. All she does is shake her head and give me a wobbly smile. I point at her, my voice shaky. "That needs to stop before I start."

I quickly realise she's not the only one. Greg's eyes glisten with unshed tears, both Sam and Mum are sniffling quietly. Even Roimata, staunch as she is, has a little water works going on.

"Okay, guys." I clap my hands, stepping into the hall as they part for me. "It's a wedding, not a funeral." But I swipe at my own eyes all the same.

Dad offers me the crook of his arm, patting my hand. "I think I heard the car pull around. Shall we?"

Hellhounds MC

Chapter Thirty-One

Matio

It didn't feel real until about five minutes ago when people started showing up and Aldrin left to pick up Marty and Barb. He's going to shit a brick when he sees the car coming to get him.

Ma and Nita have completely transformed the carpark of Lawson's Lugs, the only place we could think of on short notice that could accommodate my growing family. To be honest, I'm glad it's here instead of Ma's backyard. This is where Barb and I met, after all.

The cars have been moved from the lot, and white seats are set out on either side of a makeshift aisle.

They've laid a thin strip of carpet down the centre and they've put up an archway of small flowers. It's simple, not flashy.

Ma reaches up to brush something from my shoulder. She smiles, patting my cheek. "You ready?"

"Nervous as shit, but yeah."

She cackles. "That's normal, my boy. Once you see her though, all your nerves will disappear. That I can promise you."

She takes her seat at the front, with Nita on one side and a space for Anaru and Shaz on the other. Holden and Zeb walk down the aisle towards me.

"Jesus, look at you." Holden smirks. "You almost pass as presentable."

Holding my arms out, I give a twirl. "Not too bad, right?"

"I'd do you," Zeb says with a shrug.

"You'd do anyone, so that doesn't mean shit."

"Ooh." He thrusts both hands into his chest. "Straight for the heart, man. Harsh."

"You sayin' I'm wrong?" I quirk a brow in his direction, knowing full well I'm right.

He cocks his head with a grin. "If it walks, talks, and shows an interest, why the hell not? I'll give anything a go once. Of course, if Cami gave in and just let it happen, I wouldn't need anyone else."

Holden scowls. "Never gonna happen."

"Yee of little faith." Zeb thumps his chest. "In the words of Wayne Campbell, *she will be mine, oh yes, she will be mine.*"

"Jesus Christ, you're a loose unit. Keep on dreaming, brother." Holden slaps him on the back, and I can tell he used more force than necessary. He's always been protective over Cami, and Zeb is going to have to learn it the hard way if he keeps up his pursuit.

"Hey guys." Cassian comes up from behind. "The music is all set and ready to go. Bar is stocked too."

"Thanks, man, I appreciate it." I glance around the masses. "You here alone?" I ask slowly.

He huffs out a sigh. "Yeah, I broke it off with her. You were right."

"We've all been there, mate."

Holden scoffs. "Speak for yourself. I've only ever had eyes for Darce."

"Yeah, well, not everyone can be as lucky as you, can they?" I nod behind him. "Speaking of which."

Darcy rounds the corner in a short green dress and her hair piled on top of her head. She pushes her glasses up on her face, and it's obvious when she spots Holden, because her whole damn face lights up.

"Be right back." He's off in a jog to see her before he even finishes the sentence.

"Whipped," Zeb says with a laugh.

"And if it was Cami doing the whipping?"

"Oh, I'd be on my fucking knees worshipping her." It's so matter-of-fact that I actually believe him. Mabe this infatuation he has with her is legit and not just to piss off Holden. "Looks like we're about to start, bro." He nods to the corner of the building, where Jeri kisses Sam before heading my way. Suddenly, my palms are sweaty and I feel like I might throw up.

195

"Good luck, man." Zeb takes a seat behind Ma, as Anaru strides towards me with a warm smile. He offers his hand, pulling me into a hongi. "Nervous?" he asks when we pull apart.

"Like you wouldn't believe. I think I might be sick."

He chuckles, slapping a hand onto my shoulder. "You'll be fine. It'll pass." He shakes my hand again, then joins Ma in the front row. The rest of the family seems to have slipped in too. Jen catches my eye, giving me a thumbs up.

Holden takes his spot to my side. "You've got this, bro."

I huff out a breath, and as the music starts, I turn.

Sam comes in first, walking slowly down the aisle. My nerves crack up a notch.

As she takes her place on the other side of me, there's a pause in the music, and then there she is. Flanked by her parents, Barb steps out from around the corner and takes my fucking breath away. Ma was right.

I can't take my eyes off her.

When she reaches the front, Sandra kisses her cheek then joins the congregation. Marty kisses her other cheek and leads her up to me, passing her hand over. "Take good care of my baby girl, okay?"

"I will."

He nods and joins Sandra, then everyone takes a seat. The celebrant speaks, but I don't hear a word of it. It takes everything in me not to pull her into my arms and kiss her like no one's watching. Goddamn. I can't believe she's here, marrying me. I must be the luckiest son of a bitch there is.

Somehow, I manage to pull myself together enough to respond and say the words I need to, and just before the most important part, there's a commotion and the fast clip clop of heels running across the lot.

"Wait!" Jodi cries out, racing down the aisle towards us, Cass following close behind.

No fucking way.

"Jodi, stop," he hisses, all traces of lust gone from his expression.

"Stop the ceremony! You can't marry her!"

Barb groans. "This bitch won't quit."

"You're not welcome here." Jeri moves in to block her, and Cass falls to her other side, grabbing her arm.

"Anyone can come to a wedding," she sneers.

"Not a Hellhounds one, they can't."

"Yeah, no mutts allowed." Barb folds her arms across her chest, a steely glare aimed at Jodi.

"This is private property." Jeri nods to Zeb, who has sidled up beside her. He takes hold of her other arm. "You're trespassing."

"But... but..." Her eyes seem to dart about, searching for divine inspiration, I guess. "I'm pregnant!" she blurts, a smug smile on her face. "And you're the father." She points at me.

"What?" Cassian's eyes flick to mine, and I shake my head. He has to know I would never do that, to him or to Barb.

"What a crock of shit." Barb laughs, stepping forward, not a doubt in her mind. Fuck I love this woman. "You had your chance, and you blew it. Matiu is *my* man, and that's *never* going to change. Deal with it."

Cass pulls himself together. "Is it mine?"

Jodi spins to face him, and it's like she only just realised he was there. "Oh, hey baby," she coos.

He holds his hand up. "Is. It. Mine?"

She seems to think about it, her eyes once again dancing around the room. "I…"

"Pfftt, there's no baby," Roimata spits. "She's lying through her teeth."

Cassian's hands ball at his sides. "Get her out of here."

Jericho gives the nod, and Zeb escorts her back down the aisle where she came from, her protests ringing through the air.

"Right." Barb flicks a tendril of hair aside. "Where were we?"

We exchange rings and vows, and then, finally, I take her in my arms and press my lips to hers.

We turn to face the cheering crowd as man and wife, and at the back comes a loud yell, one that makes us stop and listen.

Wiremu stands, a pukana on his face, his stance wide. Anaru, Nikau, Greg, and Jordan all stand too, as do the rest of the cousins. Pride swells in my chest as together, they perform a haka, with Maia, Ari, and Roimata joining in vocally. Their voices rise, and I can feel the mana, the love. After all these years of not knowing who I am and where I belong, I know now. It's here, with Barb, my Hellhound brothers, and my newfound family. These are my people. This is my home.

A NOTE FROM THE AUTHOR

Thank you so much for taking the time to read *Let Loose*. This one was a long time coming! Starting a new full time job at the library and adding study into the mix, took a toll on my writing time, but we got there in the end!

Hopefully you enjoyed reading it as much as I enjoyed writing it. If you did, I would love it if you could leave a review. Reviews not only help our work to be seen, they also offer valuable feedback.

Once again, thank you for reading!

Stacey xxx

ACKNOWLEDGEMENTS

As per usual, I have to thank my girl, Trina. Like Matiu, you've always got my back. Thank you for making sure my words flow and make sense. I hate that you're leaving me. I'm gonna miss you big time!

Roimata, thank you for lending me your ear. I really appreciate you taking the time to answer my questions and chat with me. I only hope I've done your character justice.

Bestie Greg, I told you I'd write you in!

Mrs Moa, Kelly, Juanita, Molly, Janelle, Allie, Emma, Sian, Soph, Bella and all the other Booktok and Bookstagram girlies who share mine and other NZ authors' books, I love you guys! Thank you for being the push I needed to get this one finished! Especially you and your messages, Allie.

Debs, my partner in crime. I can't tell you how much I appreciate our fortnightly catch ups to write. I don't think I would've got this done without you keeping me on track.

Eli, my son and tech guru! Thank you for dropping everything and coming to fix my computer when it crashed so I *could* finish this book!

Nicole, my fellow writing procrastinator. We've had a shocking year but look at us now! We've got this!

Aaron, Bella, and River, thank you for allowing me the time to keep writing while also wrangling my studies and full-time work. It's been a year of change and upheaval, but the juggling has paid off. Your words of encouragement on both my study and reaching my writing goals have kept me going.

Last, but certainly not least, thank you to my readers. Thank you for coming on this crazy journey with me and allowing me to write the books I want to, regardless of genre. I love that you'll follow me down whatever path I choose.

ABOUT THE AUTHOR

Stacey Broadbent is a multi-genre author from New Zealand. She writes under three different names and a variety of genres, so there is something to suit most tastes. You can find her LGBTQIA reads under the name Cyan Tayse, and children's books under the name Stacey Jayne.

An avid reader and lover of all things bookish, Stacey has made it her goal to share about her favourite authors and books she's read, while also building her own publishing story. She is a qualified proofreader and is embarking on a new journey of study - Library and Information Skills.

She is a member of the Unhinged Kiwi Booktalk discord group, and a great bunch of Canterbury based bookstagrammers. Her TBR is never-ending, and though she struggles to keep up with it, she continues to add more.

As well as reading, her hobbies include LEGO, cross-stitch, crochet, and diamond art, and you can often find her sharing about her latest project on TikTok.

If you feel like stalking her, here are the links!

www.staceybroadbent.com/
www.facebook.com/StaceyBroadbentAuthor
www.amazon.com/author/staceybroadbent
Goodreads: https://goo.gl/YJ6dXa
www.instagram.com/authorstaceybroadbent/
www.bookbub.com/authors/stacey-broadbent
www.tiktok.com/@authorstaceybroadbent

OTHER BOOKS BY STACEY BROADBENT

Standalone
Never Judge a Book
Emma
Deep Heat
Lady Luck: A Deep Heat bonus novella
Fever
A Christmas Tail
Broken
Awesome Applesauce

A Step in Time series
Dancing through the Storm
Dancing in Circles
Dancing with Destiny
A Step in Time: the complete series

Super Mum series
Frazzled
Frazzled and Frumpy
Frazzled, Frumpy and Fabulous!
Super Mum: the complete series

Dark sins novellas
Sins of the Flesh
Mine

Hellhounds MC
Cut Loose
Break Loose
Let Loose

Short Stories and Poetry
Musings, Mournings, and Misadventures
Musings, Mayhem, and Mystery
Musings, Magic, and Mischief
Musings of a Writer: the complete collection

Anthologies
Scars to your Beautiful
Witching Hour: Vices and Virtues
The White Ribbon Collection
Key to my Heart
A Touch of Inspiration
No Place Like Home
Serendipity
Lucky Star
Hellhounds